Jonah disappeared as if he'd been sucked into the ground.

Valerie whipped around in search of him. Jonah was near her feet, his body sunk in the glacier. He was grasping desperately at the snow, everything below his chest disappearing into a crevasse under his feet. His face showed shock as he tried to keep himself from falling even farther.

Val threw herself to the ground, thrusting her ice ax into the snow in front of her in self-arrest position.

"Is your lead rope knotted securely?" she called.

Jonah gave her a strained "Yeah." He clearly couldn't reach his ax or help her at all.

Val tested her ax, then began looping the rope around it to create a pulley that she could utilize to haul Jonah up. Her already tired muscles and lungs burned from lack of oxygen as she anchored herself with ice screws, carabiners and rope. If she didn't do this right, it could end disastrously...

Ali Olson is a resident of Bothell, Washington, where she is kept very busy raising three young children, though she still somehow finds a little time to write, and she's very thankful for that. She has loved reading and writing her entire life and is thrilled that she gets to share her words with others. She appreciates hearing from readers. Write to her at authoraliolson.com.

Visit the Author Profile page at Harlequin.com.

Trapped
at the Summit

ALI OLSON

LOVE INSPIRED
INSPIRATIONAL ROMANCE

LOVE INSPIRED®

INSPIRATIONAL ROMANCE

ISBN-13: 978-1-335-42704-5

Trapped at the Summit

Recycling programs for this product may not exist in your area.

This edition published by arrangement with Harlequin Books S.A.

For questions and comments about the quality of this book, please contact us at CustomerService@Harlequin.com.

Love Inspired
22 Adelaide St. West, 41st Floor
Toronto, Ontario M5H 4E3, Canada
www.LoveInspired.com

Printed in U.S.A.

Serenity Prayer
God, grant me the serenity
to accept the things I cannot change,
the courage to change the things I can,
and the wisdom to know the difference.

Jesus said unto her, I am the resurrection, and the
life: he that believeth in me, though he were dead, yet
shall he live: And whosoever liveth and believeth
in me shall never die. Believest thou this?
—*John* 11:25–26

For my baby Caitlyn.

Thank you for the joy and love you bring to my life.
I feel so lucky to be your mama, and I love you
and your siblings more than I can ever say.

Chapter One

Valerie Butler stepped off the well-worn dirt trail she had been inching along and plopped herself down on the ground, pine needles crackling underneath her. She pushed her backpack off her aching shoulders, then scooted until she could lean back against a tree trunk, closing her eyes and taking deep breaths that couldn't seem to fill her lungs. As much as she breathed, she felt like she wasn't getting enough air. There was pain in her knees and ankles, and her legs felt like jelly. She couldn't even gather the energy to wipe her sweaty hair out of her face. She felt utterly defeated.

She knew she wasn't that far from the top of the mountain, probably less than half a mile. Plenty of people had given her encouraging remarks—You're almost there! You can do this!—on their way back down, which gave her some indication of how she must look at this point. She believed them, and she wanted to push just that little bit farther and get to the top. But there was nothing left in her. She wasn't sure how she was going to get back down, let alone make it to the top.

What had she been thinking when she suddenly decided to climb Mt. Si that morning? *I'm sad and alone and my life just came crashing down around my ears. Time to try hiking up a mountain!* Like that would somehow make things better.

But she'd been determined and had packed her little backpack with water and driven up here to do this thing that people who lived in the Pacific Northwest did. They hiked mountains for fun on weekends. And here it was, a gorgeous July weekend with no rain in sight, and she had been determined to climb a mountain.

It wasn't like she was that out of shape or anything. Why would climbing a mountain be so much worse than walking around downtown? Part of her had thought that doing this would help her feel better about life. Like accomplishing something new, something difficult, would be a win she could hold on to as she tried to rebuild the rest of her life.

But it wasn't going to be a win—that much was obvious now. It was just another failure on her shoulders, another time she wasn't enough. No wonder Brian broke off their engagement to be with Annalise, who would probably never be found sitting in the dirt, a sweaty mess, unable to get to the top of a dumb mountain.

Val rested her arms on her knees and her chin on her arms, trying to will herself not to think about Brian and Annalise again, knowing that she would anyway. It was why she was here on this ridiculous mountain in the first place, after all. She'd been at her little apartment trying to cancel the catering and the cake while her now-pointless wedding dress sat in the closet, and everything had felt too claustrophobic. That had been the start of this whole plan to conquer the Great Outdoors.

Except the Great Outdoors was conquering her.

She gave a little smile to an elderly couple as they continued up the trail as if they were taking a stroll through a park. She waited until they were past her before she buried her head in her arms and let a few tears fall.

She wanted to go home. Not to the tiny apartment she'd planned to rent until the wedding in a couple months. Home home. With her parents gone, though, that home didn't exist for her anymore. She had nowhere to go, really, but she knew she didn't belong in the Pacific Northwest, with its tall mountains and athletic eighty-year-olds.

"Hey," said a deep quiet voice, unexpectedly close to her. "Are you okay?"

Val didn't want to look up at whoever was speaking and let them see that she definitely was not okay. So she just spoke into her knees. "I'll be fine—thanks for checking," she said, giving a little thumbs-up to the unseen stranger.

She heard the man's footsteps moving away and felt a bit of regret. She was alone again, but was that what she wanted? Why couldn't she just ask for help and not force herself to take all the burden on her own?

Before she could answer any of her own questions, she heard the footsteps come back and felt whoever-it-was settle onto the ground beside her. Then she heard the rustle of a wrapper. "Would you like a granola bar?" the same voice asked her.

Val turned her head without lifting it off her knees until she could see the man sitting next to her, giving her a little encouraging smile and holding out a granola bar in a shiny green wrapper. His skin was the color of honey, his coffee-colored hair sat in tight curls on top of his head and his eyes were rich caramels watching her, waiting for her answer.

Val knew she must be pretty hungry if she was describing him as various foods, so she unfolded herself and took the proffered snack, leaning back against the tree trunk again. "Thanks," she said and took a bite. After a few seconds of silent chewing, she glanced over at him. It seemed like he was content to just sit there next to her and miss out on his own hike. She didn't want to do that to this very kind stranger, as much as she wanted some company. "You don't need to sit here with me. I'll be fine," she said.

He gave her a little smile and nodded. "You will be—I'm sure of that. But it doesn't seem like you're fine right now and could maybe use a friend. I'll leave if you really want me to go."

She didn't know what to say to that. He was right. She could use a friend right now. So she stayed quiet, and he seemed to understand because he didn't move from where he sat next to her. "Not having the best hike of your life, are you?" he asked.

She wanted to laugh and cry at the same time. "Not really, no. I guess mountains and I don't get along," she answered.

There was no reason to get into all the other reasons this hike wasn't going well with a complete stranger, even if he was obviously kind enough to stop and sit with her and be her side-of-the-mountain friend.

"Mt. Si isn't a breeze, that's for sure. But you're going to feel great when you get to the top," he said. He said it so matter-of-factly, as if her reaching the top was inevitable.

Val hated to disillusion him, but there was no other choice. She shook her head. "I'm not making it to the top. I'm not entirely sure I can even stand anymore. They might need to send a helicopter up for me." She smiled at another pair of retirees when they lifted their hands in a brief wave as they passed by.

Nothing she said seemed to dampen his spirit—he just kept smiling that little smile at her. "I think you should have more faith in yourself. Is anything broken?" He asked in such a way that it was clear he knew the answer was no. And he was going to try to use that to get her to climb this mountain.

"Yes," she answered, watching his eyebrows rise. "My ego."

The man's surprised laugh was as warm and kind as the rest of him seemed to be. "You're funny. Let's go," he said as he stood and held out his hand to her. She raised an eyebrow and didn't move. "Come on, you know you want to get to the top, and you're so close," he added, his hand still outstretched.

He was right—she did want to get to the top. His optimism and confidence were contagious. She reached up a hand to take his and pulled herself to standing, grimacing a little as she put weight on her legs. "Here," he said, unstrapping two hiking poles from his backpack, which was lying at his feet. He adjusted them to her length and handed them over. "These will help take the weight off your knees."

Before she could say anything, he had his backpack on and was holding hers. "Is it okay if I hold on to your bag? It'll be much easier if you aren't lugging this thing with you, and it's not actually built for hiking anyway. I'm sure a sore back isn't helping."

Well, of course it wasn't built for hiking. It was a cheap little backpack she used to carry her laptop to the nearest Starbucks sometimes. He waited for her okay, and when she nodded, he slipped it over one of his shoulders and stepped out on the trail.

She followed him, surprised by all that had happened in so little time. Only a couple minutes before she wasn't sure how she was going to get off this mountain, and now she was holding hiking poles and watching a man with a sweet, crooked smile, who had her backpack hanging off his shoulder so she wouldn't have to carry it to the summit.

"I'm Jonah, by the way," he said, holding out his hand.

"Val," she said, putting her hand in his for the second time in as many minutes.

"Hi, Val," he said, shaking her hand. "Now, how about we summit this mountain?"

She considered saying something sarcastic, but he was so sincere that no answer seemed like the better choice. It seemed he didn't require an answer, anyway, and off they went. They started walking together, and even though Val knew she was going slowly, Jonah didn't seem in any hurry and she didn't feel rushed at all.

It had been a weird few minutes, and Val couldn't help but comment on it. "How did you just convince me to do this? I swore I was done, and then you appeared out of nowhere."

"Maybe God knew you needed a little nudge," Jonah said.

Val decided that saying nothing was probably the best choice here, too. God had not been on her side lately, but that didn't seem like something she needed to share with this near stranger, as kind as he was.

A small group of teenagers caught up to them. Val expected the kids to pass without giving them a second glance, but instead the group slowed to walk with them. They all seemed to know Jonah. One of them, a redheaded girl who was probably fifteen, said, "Mr. Aarons, why're you going so slow? I expected you to run up this thing."

Val watched Jonah. He shrugged and smiled. "Why would I run? It's a beautiful day for a walk and to chat with a friend, don't you think?"

The girl rolled her eyes, but her smile made it clear she thought the world of this Mr. Aarons. "Whatever

you say. We'll see you up there!" she said, and she
gave him a little wave as the group continued on up
at a faster pace than Val could imagine at this point.
And they were *laughing*. As if climbing mountains
was just a fun thing you did sometimes.

She really didn't understand the Pacific Northwest.

Val looked at Jonah with eyebrows raised. "So,
you're a camp counselor or something who regularly
runs up mountains, huh?"

Jonah laughed again, and Val had to smile. He
had a great laugh. "I'm a youth pastor, here with a
group from my church, and running up a mountain
is pretty rare. But I do spend a fair amount of time
climbing them."

Val could tell by the ease and strength with which
he carried both their backpacks along the switchbacks that he was more than capable of running up
a mountain. But he didn't seem at all perturbed with
the pace. In fact, he seemed as pleased as could be
to be walking with her. His presence was soothing.
She imagined the kids would feel comfortable sharing their problems with this man.

"Shouldn't you be herding them up this mountain instead of me?" she asked, trying not to gasp.

"We have a pretty small group and there are two
other chaperones here. Right now, my job is to get
myself to the top of the mountain so I can meet

up with them there, and that's exactly what we're doing," he told her.

Jonah said it as if it was a sure thing they were going to make it to the summit together, and it gave Val another boost of energy. She enjoyed this man's confidence in her.

"So that's why *I'm* on this mountain today. How about you?" he asked her.

"Oh, I do this every weekend," she said, partly because she didn't want to talk about what had brought her there, but mostly just so she could hear his laugh again.

Her efforts were rewarded, and she smiled at him. "Fair enough," he said. "What do you do on the rare day you aren't climbing Mt. Si?"

"I work at a publishing house," she said, only realizing after the words were out that that wasn't exactly true.

She *had* worked at a publishing house. Back in St. Louis. But she'd quit so she could move here to be with Brian when he got a job in Seattle. Now she had no job as well as no fiancé.

"Want to talk about it?" he asked, his voice soft again, seeming to understand that her job wasn't as safe a topic as he had originally assumed.

No, she didn't want to talk about it. Definitely not.

"I just moved here a couple of months ago," she

said. "Quit my job and packed everything up and moved across the country to marry someone who broke up with me three days ago so he could date a woman I'd asked to be one of my bridesmaids."

She didn't know what had made her say all that, but she felt a little better for it, even as the tears started again. She felt a little less alone.

There was a brief pause before he said, "So not your best week ever then, huh?"

She laughed and sobbed at the same time. "Nope, you didn't catch me in a banner year, that's for sure."

They walked a little longer in silence. Val knew she shouldn't have thrown all that at this person she had just met, and now she wasn't sure what else to say. It seemed like an odd time to talk about normal banalities like the weather.

Jonah stopped walking and so did she, but she was too caught up in her own thoughts to notice where she was. His voice broke into her thoughts. "Well, I don't know if this makes you feel any better, but you did just manage to summit Mt. Si."

Val looked around and realized she was on a flat expanse of land crowded with groups of people admiring the view. She felt her heart swell a little as she looked behind her, at those last few switchbacks she had covered to get herself to the top. Then she looked ahead and saw a clear view of nearby mountains and tiny houses. "I can't believe I made it," she told Jonah, feeling a bit of pride in herself.

He gave her a mischievous grin. "Oh, we're not finished yet."

She shrugged. "Yeah, but going back down won't be nearly as miserable, will it?" she asked. It had been surprisingly difficult for her to get up there, so she had to assume the way back would be comparatively a piece of cake.

"You can't go back down before climbing the haystack."

Val shook her head. "I don't know what the haystack is, but no more climbing. I already made it to the top."

Jonah pointed over at a pile of rocks people were scrambling up and down. "That's the tippy-top. Don't you want to go to the tippy-top of the mountain? You've already made it this far."

Val considered being stubborn and saying no, she didn't particularly want to go to the tippy-top, thank you very much. But his enthusiasm and encouragement made her refusal die on her tongue. She paused for a moment and looked at him, then at the rocks again.

"Tippy-top it is," she said, stretching her arms and legs.

The smile he gave her lit up his entire face, and she knew she'd made the right choice. "You picked an amazing day for this hike," he told her as they started at the bottom of the haystack. "You hardly ever get such a good view from up here. Usually you're just looking at clouds."

"How many times have you been up here?" she asked, trying to distract herself from her tired muscles.

"Dozens," he said.

"Dozens! Are you joking?" she asked. She took her first tentative step onto the rocks, holding on with her hands to keep herself steady. Jonah climbed beside her, looking comfortable and sure of himself, just as he had since they'd met.

"Nope. I take a group up here a few times every summer, plus coming up with friends sometimes. And I've lived in this area my whole life. I remember climbing these rocks with my mom and dad when I was maybe ten years old."

"And you're not bored of it?" she asked, looking for a handhold to pull herself over a particularly large boulder.

He held out a hand to help her. She grasped it tightly and scrambled up to the next part. His arms were strong and steady, and she thought it was funny how quickly she had come to trust this man she'd only just met.

"Nope, not bored at all. I've climbed nearly everything around here, but Mt. Si feels like my home mountain. It's wonderful every time."

Another few seconds of scrambling and they were there. She sat down and looked around. "And now I'm at the tippy-top," she said.

"Knew you could do it," he told her with that same happy confidence as he sat down next to her.

They sat there for a little while, looking out at the valley below. Val couldn't believe she'd managed to make it so far. She basked in the sun and this feeling of accomplishment.

Jonah looked out at the view from the top of the haystack, but he hardly saw it. He wanted to keep looking at the woman next to him, studying her expression as she took in their surroundings and rested on the rocks. See her jade green eyes again, study how her long, loose russet curls framed her face.

And if there was any way to cause her to beam at him like she had when they'd made it to the top of the rocks, he wanted to do it, because that smile struck him in a way he couldn't explain. She was absolutely beautiful when she smiled, but it was even more than that. Her soul seemed to shine through her face when she was smiling, and it took his breath away.

But from the little she'd said about her past few days, she didn't need someone staring at her or feeling what he felt when he was near her. So instead he looked out at the view and said a prayer.

Thank You, God, for putting her in my path.

From just the short time they'd already spent together, she had made his day better. Not that it had been a bad day to begin with. It'd been pretty great, in fact. But meeting her took it up an extra few notches.

And he hoped he was making hers better, too. Comparing the sparkle in her eyes and the little up-turn of her lips as she sat there on the top of the haystack to how she'd been when he first met her by the side of the trail, he was pretty sure he had. He couldn't imagine a sadder sight than this woman curled up on the ground, her arms wrapped around her legs, head on her knees, as if she was all alone in the world and completely worn down by it. The moment he'd seen her, he'd known she needed a friend and some encouragement.

And now here she was at the top of the haystack, looking across God's glory.

As if on cue, she turned toward him, and the smile she gave him sent a wave of emotions through him. He wanted to capture this moment so he could remember it for the rest of his life.

Which reminded him.

"I know this might be a weird request, but would you take a picture with me?"

There was a brief pause while she seemed to process the question, then answered uncertainly, "I guess."

"It's for my sister," he explained. "I always take pictures for her when I'm on hikes. It's a thing we do."

Val shifted a little closer and Jonah set his phone to selfie mode. He quickly snapped a picture of the two of them together atop the haystack. He knew Becca would want to know about the woman in the picture, and he smiled to think about the conversation they'd have about this experience. It would probably be a pretty intense interrogation, if he knew his sister.

He put his phone away. "Thanks, Val. That'll make her happy. She gets very annoyed if I forget."

She nodded. "Thank you for helping me get here," she said.

"You're welcome," he answered. "But you were the one who did it. I just gave you that last little push, and I credit God with that one."

Her smile turned a little constrained, and he could see the pain in her eyes. He was considering whether it was better to ask her about it or not when she spoke. "God hasn't exactly been on my side lately," she said, looking away again.

Jonah could feel the pain she was experiencing as she said that. He wasn't sure what to say, but he knew he had to help if he could. "I know you've been going through a really hard time. But He's always on your side, even if it doesn't seem like it. I don't think He's given you anything you can't handle."

She still seemed skeptical. He gestured to the trail they'd just walked. "Like this mountain. It was tough and felt almost impossible there for a bit, but you did it and now here you are."

Val didn't say anything and stared out at the view. She seemed to be mulling over his words. He hoped they would give her comfort. She was clearly in need of some comfort. He was prepared to sit with her there as long as she needed. After all, he knew how important it was sometimes to just have a person with you. That was one of the special things about having a twin, and he never took it for granted.

Then he noticed the group of teens and chaperones gathering below the haystack and knew he needed to join them and make sure everyone was there and doing okay. He was torn about what to do, but only for a moment. Then he turned to her.

"I need to go talk to my group," he told her, gesturing to the teenagers standing a few yards away.

If he had been planning on saying goodbye then, the look in her eyes would have made it impossible.

As it was, he didn't even want to go those few yards. But he knew what he needed to do. "It'll only take a couple of minutes. Will you wait for me? I'd like to walk down with you. A little company makes hiking so much better. And those trekking poles will be useful if your legs aren't used to the downhill, but I'm going to want them back."

The thing about his poles was only a little true—he did love those poles—but they were far from the only reason he wanted to walk down the mountain with her. It seemed enough for her, though, because she nodded. "Great. Just wait for me for a few minutes," he said.

"Trust me, I won't be going anywhere fast for days," she joked.

He laughed and scrambled down to his group, his mind still beside her on top of the rocks. Even only knowing Val such a short time, he was more than certain he'd never met anyone quite like her, and he couldn't wait to spend the next couple hours learning more.

He counted heads and confirmed that everyone had made it safely and felt okay to descend, reminded them all of the safety procedures and sent them on their way back down. Before they left, he pulled aside one of the other chaperones, Nick, who also happened to be a good friend. "I might be a little slow getting down. If everyone's accounted for, send me a message letting me know and head back to camp, okay? I'll get there when I can."

Nick looked concerned. "Is someone hurt? Are *you* hurt?"

Jonah wasn't surprised at Nick's reaction. Jonah was usually right there with the kids. Honestly, he could run down this thing and make it back to camp long before anyone else showed up if he wanted to.

Jonah shook his head and smiled to reassure his friend. "No, no injuries. There's a woman I met on the way up who could use a friend right now. I'm going to walk down with her, see if I can ease her troubles a little."

Jonah glanced over at Val, who was still sitting on the haystack, and she gave him a little wave and started carefully making her way back down the rocks. She grimaced a little as she stretched her legs, and Jonah knew she was going to have a hard time walking for the next few days. But she seemed so much happier than when they'd met, and her expression was more determined than exhausted.

"She's pretty," Nick commented, giving Jonah a glance.

Jonah wanted to roll his eyes. His friends at church had all convinced themselves that they needed to help find him a girlfriend, so he immediately saw where this was going. He hated to burst Nick's bubble, and in fact didn't much like the truth of the situation himself, but it was what it was.

"She just had a messy breakup with her fiancé," he explained. "I doubt she'll be going on dates anytime soon. She's got enough on her plate without that. I certainly wouldn't be so callous as to ask her out right now."

That comment wasn't just for Nick, and Nick's little smirk told Jonah that it was obvious to him, too. There was a lot unsaid, and they were good enough friends to both recognize it all.

They both knew, for example, that Jonah would love to ask Val out on a date. Even these few short interactions had been enough to make him sure of that. But he was also sure that she just needed a friend, and that was what he would be.

So he said goodbye to Nick, who started on the descent with the last of the campers, and then went over to help Val. She was almost off the haystack, scooting down the last big boulder carefully. He held out a hand and she grabbed it, hopping the last couple feet until she was standing beside him. She grimaced again and stretched her legs. Yep, she was going to be sore the next day. He handed her his trekking poles. "You ready to try downhill?" he asked.

"Ready," she told him, shivering a little. "Let's get off this mountain. I'm freezing."

"Do you have a jacket in your backpack?" he asked, guessing the answer and starting to rummage in his own bag.

She shook her head like that was a crazy thing to expect of her. "It was almost ninety degrees when I left my apartment."

Jonah smiled as he gave her the one he always had in his bag for exactly this reason, which she took without argument. "Mountains are different. The elevation keeps the summits chilly all year round. You should always pack at least a little something."

"I'll remember that next time," she said with a little sarcastic smirk that said *I'll never be doing this again, trust me.*

He smiled at her. "You might be surprised at yourself. The mountains around here are amazing, and there are so many of them. Maybe this will become your new favorite pastime," he told her.

She chuckled. "That's a lot of optimism there, Jonah," she told him.

He shrugged. "Optimism is kind of my thing," he said.

Val pulled on the jacket and wrapped it tight around herself. He had an urge to wrap his arms around her, too, and share some of his warmth, but instead he picked up their packs and she grabbed the trekking poles from where she'd leaned them against the rocks. "Moving will help warm you up, too," he said, turning toward the trail, his heart thumping a little harder than it should have.

He didn't want to like her, but he did anyway. It was as simple as that. He knew he wouldn't be able to do anything about it, and he already regretted that, but he'd enjoy this time and accept that this was just a friendly hike and nothing more. They started making their way down the mountain.

They only walked in silence for a few seconds before Val started talking. "Are there other mountains around here you regularly climb to the tippy-top of?" she asked.

"Oh yeah," he said, excited to share one of his favorite topics with her. "The Cascades are full of great hikes. That's the mountain range here. You can also go to the peninsula and hike the Olympics," he explained. "There are so many beautiful places up here."

He watched her, surprised she was even interested. But she nodded and asked, "What's the hardest mountain you've hiked?"

He wasn't sure why she wanted to know. Perhaps she was just trying to fill the silence or keep from thinking too much. Whatever the reason, he was happy to oblige. "Mt. Rainier is brutal. The elevation, glaciers and crazy weather patterns combine to make it extremely difficult for even the most seasoned mountaineer. I've attempted it five times and have only made it to the summit twice."

"And that's fun for you?" she asked, sounding as if she thought he might be slightly insane.

He nodded, grinning. "It really is. There's something great about pushing your body that far, seeing what you can do, fighting against the elements. And it's so beautiful. Really, you're living in the best part of the country."

She chuckled. "I can see why you're a youth pastor. You're very chipper."

He nodded. "I can't help it. God has given me so much."

"I used to be chipper," she mumbled, as if talking to herself.

He knew he didn't need to answer. She probably didn't expect him to. Still, he couldn't let her sit in that mood without saying anything. "I'm sure you can get there again. Just look at how much you have to be grateful for. I'm certain the list is very long if you think about it," he said in a soft voice.

He watched her think about his words and hoped she would take them kindly, the way he meant them, and truly consider what he'd said. He could see a lighthearted nature in her, but it was covered over with sadness and mistrust in the world. He hoped a little time would help her wounds heal and bring out that happier version of her. This one was already amazing, and he was pretty sure that other one would be jaw-dropping.

He noticed where they were on the hike and smiled to himself.

"Here's one example," he said, gesturing to her to follow him a little off the trail. A minute later, they were standing beside a little stream of water, tree trunks covered in moss surrounding them. Everything was green and sparkling and fresh. "I love this spot," he said, putting his hand on one of the trees. "It feels like a little part of the world that's still untouched by humans."

They stood there for a short time, silently enjoying the beauty of the place. Then they smiled at each other and continued on their way down. Jonah glanced over at her and saw that she looked thoughtful but still had that slump to her shoulders that told him she was carrying a burden.

He wasn't sure if it was okay to ask about Val's broken engagement or if it would put her in an uncomfortable position, but he could see it was weighing on her. "Do you want me to talk more about mountains?" he asked, wondering if she would appreciate the distraction.

The look of relief on her face made it clear he'd hit the nail on the head. "Yes, I'd love to hear about them," she replied.

So he told her more about the local hikes and places she should go. He just talked, filling up the empty space with stories and details of this beautiful area he'd lived in his entire life. After a little while he could see a smile on her face, and finally she started to giggle.

Jonah raised his eyebrow at her, wondering what was going on in her head.

"You're a mountaineering minister," she said. He waited and she tried to explain. "I've clearly been away from my job for too long because my brain started making up book titles for you. Like *The Mountaineering Minister* and *The Secret of Curly's Cave*," she told him, painting the title across the sky with one hand.

It was such an unexpected thing for her to say, he couldn't help but laugh. "I'll need to tell Becca about that. Maybe she'll write it for me," he said.

"Is Becca your sister?" Val asked.

"Yeah. We're twins, so we're pretty close. And she loves to write. I'm sure she'd get a kick out of turning me into her own version of Nancy Drew."

Val chuckled. He loved the sound of it and wondered how long it had been since she'd truly laughed, a loud full guffaw. He hoped he could get one out of her by the end of their hike.

But she soon sobered, and Jonah knew that there would be no guffaw right this moment. He waited to see if she would tell him what had changed her mood so quickly. "I'll need to start looking for a new job, as soon as I figure out where I'm going to live."

Ah. He could see why she might feel lost right now. "Do you think you'll move back home?" he asked. The selfish part of him hoped she was planning to stay.

"I don't know," she answered with a shrug. "I moved to St. Louis three years ago because my fiancé lived there. Then he got a job out here and I followed him, and I'd just gotten settled and started my job search when I found out about him and Annalise. I haven't really had a home since I was a little kid, and I'm not going to move back there, as much as I miss it sometimes."

He could see a couple of tears slip down her cheeks and could feel the hurt in her words. It seemed like she had even more going on than the broken engagement. "Can I just say, you are pretty amazing," he said.

She gave him a look of surprise. "Why do you say that?"

She seemed genuinely to not know. It was shocking to him that she didn't see it.

"You've clearly been through so much, and yet

here you are," he explained, gesturing around them. "Still going, trying something new, moving forward. That's amazing."

She seemed a little skeptical, even though it was obvious to him. Jonah continued, "You could be at home curled up in a ball and nobody would blame you."

"But I decided to do that on the side of a mountain in front of a bunch of strangers," she concluded with a little grimace.

Jonah shook his head. He couldn't believe she didn't see what he saw. "And then you got back up and you kept going."

"With some help," she told him pointedly.

Jonah shrugged off his contribution. "We all need help sometimes," he said. "You were willing to accept that help and do something pretty cool. Plus, you were almost there. I believe you would've gotten to the top eventually even without me."

There was a long pause while she seemed to digest everything he'd said, and then the conversation turned to lighter topics. Val told him more about her old job and what she was looking for in her next one. Her passion and interest in language was evident, and it sounded like fascinating work when she described it. He hoped she would find another position she loved so much.

"And you're a youth pastor," she said. "What's that like?"

"It's great," he said. "I really enjoy helping with the kids. But I only do that on the weekends."

"So the rest of the week, you're a billionaire philanthropist?"

He laughed. She made him laugh so easily. "A firefighter, which suddenly sounds much less impressive," he said.

"So you save kids on the weekend and cats stuck in trees Monday through Friday? That's almost more impressive than being Batman," she said.

He laughed. She was clever. "That's one way of looking at it, yeah," he said. "But I don't think I've got anything on Batman."

"I don't know. On the rare occasion, you even save women stuck on the sides of mountains," she added.

"Well, that happens more often than you might think, actually," he said.

She laughed. A real, full surprised laugh that bubbled up from inside her and seemed to make the whole world just a little bit brighter. It was over quickly, but he couldn't seem to wipe the foolish grin off his face. He thanked God again for putting Val in his path.

Jonah noticed the time slipping away as they continued their hike. Val seemed to have no trouble going downhill, and they were making great progress as they talked. Soon they were only a mile away from the trailhead and probably saying goodbye forever. Jonah felt a little disappointed. He wished they were going a bit slower, that the time would last.

Because he already knew he wouldn't be asking for her number. And though she was friendly and had laughed with him, she was someone who had been dumped by her fiancé that week and was considering moving a thousand miles away. He had no illusions that he'd ever see this woman again.

So he put his energy into enjoying the time they had left together, and they talked and laughed the rest of the way down the mountain. Later he couldn't remember exactly what they discussed, but he could recall every smile she gave him, every bubble of laughter.

When they reached the trailhead and the parking lot, Jonah handed Val her backpack and she gave him back his trekking poles. "You did it," he told her with an encouraging smile. "You climbed a whole big mountain. You can do anything you put your mind to—I'm sure of that much."

Val's green eyes pierced him right to his soul. "Thank you," she said again, though he could tell that this time she was talking about more than just his push to get her to the summit.

"You're welcome," he said with a smile.

They lingered for a few seconds, but Jonah had nothing else to say, so he just waited to see what would happen next. Val seemed to be wondering the same thing, but when the silence went unbroken, she dipped her eyes to her backpack and pulled out a set of keys. "Enjoy the rest of your time at camp," she told him, holding out her hand.

He shook it, enjoying the feel of her hand in his. "And best of luck figuring out the future. I hope all the best for you."

They let go, and she was about to turn away when Jonah added, "God's got your back, you know."

Val gave him a little smile he couldn't quite read. "I think you might be right about that," she said, and then she was gingerly settling into her small silver car, giving him a grimace and a laugh because of her sore muscles. A few seconds later the door was closed, the engine was on and she was turning out of the parking lot.

Jonah had a crazy urge to chase after the vehicle and ask her for a number, an email address, something so he could keep her from disappearing from his life forever.

But then the car was gone, and he took a deep breath. *God has a plan*, he reminded himself, before starting on the short walk back to camp.

Chapter Two

One year later

Val stood just outside of the rudimentary stone hut of Camp Muir, her arms crossed over her chest to help keep in her body's warmth despite the frigid temperature. Even though it was August, it was freezing at this elevation, especially in the middle of the night. But she didn't want to go inside to grab her jacket, possibly disturbing the other hikers and her sick friend, Ellie, in the process. She'd stay out and be cold while taking in the view for a few more minutes before going back inside, checking on Ellie and getting some more sleep if she could.

It was dark and Val couldn't see much with just the moon for light, but it was enough to show a bit of the desolate landscape that had taken her breath away the day before. Stark and treeless, but beautiful in its own way, a sheet of ice that spread out and up, with dark patches of rock occasionally breaking through. There was nothing else this far up, no trees or animals. Just one little hut where a few hikers were sleeping, the ice and rocks, and her.

She had read so much about Mt. Rainier, spent most of the winter gathering information and creating a plan to get strong enough to complete the hike to the top. She knew all the ins and outs of the trip. But finally being at this point for the first time sent a wave of awe through her that nothing could have prepared her for, even as she dealt with the disappointment that this was as far as she would be able to go. For today, possibly forever. She looked at the snow in front of her, with the moonlight reflecting off it, and mentally ran through what it would take to get to the top: a hike across Cowlitz Glacier, through Cathedral Gap, up The Flats, along Disappointment Cleaver, to High Break, and then Columbia Crest and the summit.

She'd studied, practiced and prepped, and now here she was, unable to go any farther. Even just the very first section, the Cowlitz Glacier, looked dangerous and unforgiving, and she wanted so much to walk across it and find out what she was capable of. The thought of turning back now, after everything she had done to get ready for this over the past year, made her eyes fill with tears.

She sent up a little prayer of hope. "Lord, help me find a way," she whispered.

She didn't want this to be her only chance and hoped it wouldn't be, but she knew there was a possibility this could be her last opportunity to climb a tall mountain. Val was only twenty-eight and outwardly looked healthier than she ever had at any other point in her life. But she knew she might never have another opportunity to conquer such a challenge, and she couldn't quite convince herself that she was going to go home without attempting it. Her dream to summit Rainier was too powerful, too important to just give up.

She began going through her options. Hiking alone wouldn't be safe, but maybe she could find another group and join them, if they could be convinced that she wouldn't be a liability. That was the only way she'd be able to hike this morning, and she would cling to that hope.

Val heard the movement of other hikers and moved aside to allow them to pass through the door, wondering if this first group would be sympathetic to her plight. Five people filed past her, stretching and appearing groggy as they prepared to begin their ascent. It was unsurprising that they were struggling a little; they'd probably had about as much sleep as she had. Lots of hikers chose to start Rainier in the middle of the night, though, to avoid descending during the heat of midday and risking the crevasses and other dangers that occurred when the snow melted.

They spoke to each other quietly, adjusting headlamps and tying lead ropes. Val took a breath, ready to ask them to let her join their group. She'd beg and bribe if necessary, anything to get the chance to summit.

Before she could start toward them, however, she heard more rustling in the doorway and watched a man duck through the frame that was too short for his large figure. He was tall, with a body that showed the fitness of a mountaineer. Or maybe even a firefighter.

Val forgot about the other group as she felt a wave of familiarity. She watched as he looked through his pack, going through his own preparations. She tried not to get her hopes up that it was the person she'd been watching for on every hike over the past year—what were the chances it was him?—but she watched carefully nonetheless. Nobody else joined him, and he obviously wasn't a part of that other group, which had already begun their journey. It was difficult to believe, but it seemed like he was preparing to go out alone, something she couldn't imagine anyone doing on this dangerous mountain. As he turned to lift his pack, the moonlight revealed his face and Val felt the thrill of recognition. It *was* him. She'd hoped so much to see him again and now here he was, standing before her.

The colors of his warm brown eyes and deep tanned skin were lost in the darkness that surrounded them, but she wouldn't forget that face in her lifetime. She felt a rush of excitement and worked to keep her voice down to a half whisper when she said his name, trying to get his attention. There were a dozen or so still-sleeping hikers just a few feet away, after all.

He looked toward her, and she stepped closer so he could see her better. He seemed to struggle with what he was seeing. She had no doubt it was quite a surprise, and she looked at him, soaking him in. It had been so long. She was sure she was beaming. "Hi, Jonah. Fancy meeting you on the side of a mountain again," she said, trying to keep from outright laughing with joy.

"Val?" he asked in his own whisper, sounding completely baffled. "What are you doing here?" He looked her up and down as if he couldn't quite believe it was her.

And of course he should be surprised. It had been just over a year ago when they'd first met, and that time she'd been gasping near the top of another, much smaller mountain. She had told him she would probably be leaving the Pacific Northwest, and that she would probably never be caught climbing a mountain again.

And now here she was, at a ten-thousand-foot elevation on the side of Mt. Rainier, one of the most formidable mountains in the country. And she was well prepared to attempt a summit. She was very aware of the transformation she'd gone through since they'd last met and didn't blame him for his shock.

So much had happened in the past year. Last summer, she had been brokenhearted, out of shape and low on faith. And afraid of so many things. But completing that hike and meeting Jonah had set off a series of events in her life so profound that she hardly recognized that old version of herself. She had found a job, a home and a life in this area, and it was better than she could ever have imagined even before Brian decided not to go through with the wedding. Her soul and heart had healed, and her body had become strong and capable as she'd mastered longer and more difficult challenges, eventually leading her to this place on this day. And here he was, too.

She grinned and hugged him, feeling the same flood of warmth that she had experienced during their time together on Mt. Si. It had surprised her then—after all, she had been so hurt by Brian's betrayal and the loss of her fairy-tale wedding, it was a shock that anything could get through that wall of sadness. Still, his presence was so refreshing and wonderful that she had been disappointed when they'd separated without exchanging numbers. But at the time she'd told herself that there was no point asking for his number since she'd probably be moving anyway.

Only she hadn't, and instead she went on another hike, and then another and another and met some people, and through one of those people she found a publishing house who needed an editor. And soon she'd found herself settled but without any way to contact Jonah, the man who had started it all. So many times over the past year, she'd wished she could see him again.

So she had found herself climbing Mt. Si often and noticing each person, hoping Jonah would be on a hike there that day, too, adding to the dozens of times he'd climbed it. It was her most frequented spot for that very reason, and she could fairly run up the mountain by this time. But she had never crossed paths with him again.

And now here he was. It was as if God had been listening to her, and just when she needed to see

Jonah's face the most, He had brought them back together.

She looked into those eyes she felt like she knew so well even though she hardly knew them at all. Her smile was so wide she imagined she looked a little crazy, but it couldn't be helped. At least it was dark, she reminded herself. "It's so good to see you again," she said, knowing that those words couldn't possibly convey how happy she was at that moment.

"Val?" he asked again with a little shake of his head, seemingly still unable to understand how she could be standing there in front of him.

"Yeah, it's me," she said with a chuckle. She wanted to explain her journey to this place, but there was something more pressing on her mind and she needed to address that first. "You're not going out there alone, are you?" she asked.

When it was a stranger, she was concerned. Knowing it was Jonah, a man she held dear in her heart, she was filled with worry for his safety. He had mentioned a year ago how dangerous Rainier was, and she'd done some research herself and knew exactly the risks. The weather was unpredictable, the terrain was treacherous, there could be avalanches and earthquakes and a hundred other accidents, and having someone with you could mean the difference between life and death. He could fall into a crevasse and die because nobody would be there to rescue him. It wouldn't be the first time it had happened, and he had to know that as well as she did.

Hiking Mt. Rainier in a group was dangerous enough. Hiking it alone was playing with fire, and she wasn't going to sit by without saying anything if that was his plan. She crossed her arms and waited for his answer, feeling a little bit like a mom but not caring.

He shrugged, not looking at her. "I've done it a few times with friends. It's not a big deal. I'll be fine," he said emphatically. His voice held a note of something between anger and despair, and Val heard it clear as day. It told her that he wasn't going to give up his attempt just because she was worried for his safety. Safety didn't seem to be playing a role in his decision at all.

Her worry for him turned into something much stronger. Something was very wrong here—she could feel it.

It was hard to see in the gloom, but Val could make out strain in his expression and in the slope of his shoulders. There was a worn-down, tired look about him that hadn't been there the year before. She had been too excited to see him at first to notice it, but now that she was really looking, the change was obvious. His cheerful optimism didn't shine out of him like it had when they'd first met. Apparently she hadn't been the only one to have a life-changing year, but his clearly wasn't for the better.

She had no idea what trials he might have faced since she'd seen him last, but it was obvious that whatever they were, they had taken a toll on this man who had been so carefree and confident in the beauty of the world he inhabited. "Let me go with you," she said to him, almost before she recognized it as a conscious thought.

Jonah looked startled, but Val knew this was the perfect solution. She needed to summit, that other group had already left and Jonah needed somebody to be there for him. If he agreed to her idea, they would summit together, just like on Mt. Si, only this time it was Jonah who seemed to be struggling and in need of a little help.

She felt in her heart this was the right thing to do, and that this had to be part of God's plan for both of them. He'd been there for her in her hour of need, when she'd felt lost and alone, and now it was her turn to do the same. He still seemed skeptical, though, so she rushed to explain. "I came here with two friends, but one is sick and the other's not comfortable leaving her here alone. With the weather turning tomorrow, this is my only day to summit and I've worked so hard to prepare for it. Please let me hike with you. It would mean so much to me."

She felt like she was begging a little, but she didn't care. If he let her come because he pitied her predicament, that was fine. The important thing was that he said yes.

She didn't tell him that he shouldn't go alone; he already knew that. So Val waited, watching him, unable to look away from his face. She still couldn't believe he was actually there, right in front of her. Even if he'd changed over the past year, it was still Jonah. She'd found him again.

He hesitated, and she waited for his answer. *Please, God, help him say yes. I don't know what's wrong, but he needs both of us right now.*

Finally Jonah nodded. "Talk to your friends first, though. And if you're sure you'd like to hike with me, I'll wait."

Val's heart jumped in excitement. She grinned and gave his arm a brief squeeze before turning back toward the dark building called Camp Muir. It wasn't much more than a box, with a few shelves along the walls for people to lie down on and rest before beginning their summit attempt. Even with all her preparations, she'd been surprised at how basic it was. Now, in the middle of the night, the small building was filled with sleeping bodies, all hoping to make it to the top. She moved quietly toward her friends, not wanting to disturb those who would begin later in the morning in favor of a couple hours' more sleep.

When she reached the shelf occupied by her friend Ellie, she found Clayton sitting beside her running his fingers through her hair and talking in a soft murmur, exactly as he had been doing when Val had gone outside to breathe the fresh air and get over her disappointment. Clay seemed content to watch over her as she recovered from the altitude sickness that had racked her body, the hike and all other plans forgotten the second she began to seem sick. Ellie and Val had both thought she might recover in time, but when the poor woman had tried to get up, it was obvious there was no way she was going to attempt a summit.

They were planning on waiting until dawn and then heading back down to their cars. Val worried that she was leaving her friends in the lurch, but she also had a very good reason for wanting to give them some time alone. She would've been more inclined to stay and help her friend, except she knew this might be the perfect opportunity for something that should've happened a long time ago for those two.

Val studied her sick friend and was relieved to see she was looking a bit better. It seemed she had fallen asleep while Val was gone, though Clay apparently hadn't moved and wouldn't anytime soon, whether or not Ellie actually needed him. Val saw the tenderness in Clayton's movements as he tended to their friend, and Val's heart ached. To have someone care for her that way…

But that was a useless thought to have, especially now. She was in no spot to start a romantic relationship, even though the one man she'd thought of in that way in such a long while was standing right outside the door, waiting for her.

Val pushed those thoughts away and walked closer to Clayton so she could speak to him in whispers. Clay looked up at Val when she arrived, though he didn't stop his ministrations. It only took a few minutes to explain the situation to him. "And you two can either rest here until I get back or head down without me. I will message you as soon as I get back to Camp Muir," she finished.

Clayton looked a little worried about her, but she expected that of him by this point. He occasionally behaved like a big brother to her, which she loved, never having had that before. But after some whispered reassurances that she knew and trusted Jonah's mountaineering abilities and that she would be safe, Clayton nodded, reluctantly. "Don't be afraid to quit if it's not feeling right. There will be other chances. And we'll be here waiting for you when you get back, don't worry. I think it's best to let Ellie rest as much as possible," he said.

Val agreed and promised to see them in a few hours. She didn't know how to tell him that this might be her only shot on the mountain and she wasn't going to give up, no matter what the mountain threw at her. She knew she needed to talk to her friends about what was going on in her life, but she just couldn't find the words. She didn't want to worry her surrogate big brother until after she'd attempted Mt. Rainier, though she felt a little guilty that the closest people she had in her life didn't know about her diagnosis. But she swallowed her guilt, gave Clay a quick hug, checked her pack for her phone and GPS device, and turned to leave.

She hesitated, though. There was one more thing she needed to tell Clayton, just in case he hadn't made the decision on his own. She turned back to him. "Tell her how you feel, Clay," Val said. "This has gone on long enough. She deserves to hear what you've been thinking all this time," she said, looking at the two figures, one asleep on a little shelf, the other kneeling beside her as if she was the most precious thing in the world.

He turned toward her, and she thought he might argue or deny the truth of what she'd said, but after a few seconds she heard him sigh and his dark shape shifted back to where he'd been. He put his hand on Ellie's forehead. "I know," he answered. She thought he might say more, but he didn't, and Val was content to leave it at that.

She gave his arm an encouraging squeeze and sneaked back out, as quietly as she possibly could, to where Jonah was waiting. He was standing there, a dark shadow against the lighter snow. His pack was at his feet, and he was looking out at the mountain, just as she had been doing a few minutes ago. She hoped he was seeing its beauty and not ruminating on whatever difficulties he was experiencing, but she couldn't see him well enough to know.

"Everything's set," she told him. He nodded and they both checked their bags and bodies for the necessary safety gear.

Val put on her gloves, ensured she had her ice ax, her avalanche beacon and her cell phone. It wouldn't work on most of the mountain, but it was good to have nonetheless. An extra warm jacket for when they stopped for breaks, extra clothes, plenty of snacks and water, and various other items for emergencies. Everything was there. Then she attached her crampons so her steps would dig into the icy ground and make walking safer. She'd practiced all of this enough times that it only took a couple of minutes.

Then she tied the lead rope to her waist as she'd

been trained and handed the other end to Jonah to do the same. His movements were swift and efficient, and in no time at all they had both settled their packs into place and focused their headlamps at the ground in front of them.

Val couldn't believe that she was going to summit Mt. Rainier with the man who had started her on this journey in the first place. It was more than a coincidence, she knew, and she lifted her eyes skyward, saying a brief prayer of thanks.

Jonah looked at Val again, studying her strong body, her confident movements, not quite able to believe the current situation. Their time on Mt. Si had only been last summer, though it felt like a lifetime ago, and to see her here, now, was more than astonishing. It was downright impossible.

When they'd last met, she had looked so sad there by the side of the trail, curled up in a ball, that he hadn't been able to walk by without checking on her. What he hadn't expected was the striking jade green eyes that had sent a charge of electricity through his body and soul when she looked at him. Nor had he expected the self-deprecating smile and sense of humor that had shone through immediately.

The memory was so fresh. How they had talked

and laughed, how she had gathered enough strength to keep going, not to give up—

"Ready?" the real, present-day Val asked, startling him out of his thoughts. She shifted her pack slightly, tightened a strap and looked at him expectantly. A small breeze picked up, blowing around those same russet curls, although they were black in the darkness. She pulled them into a quick ponytail to keep them out of her face and put on her helmet.

The transformation that had occurred over a single year was astonishing. This confident and competent mountaineering woman was so different from the tired and broken one sitting on the side of another mountain. The self-deprecating smile was gone, a genuine one in its place. She exuded strength and determination, as if she trusted herself to face any challenge set before her.

His heart hurt when he thought about the transformation he'd gone through over that same time. They were both so different from who they had been when they'd last met. He could tell by the concern on her face that she'd noticed the change in him already, and he felt a little worse. She didn't even know the half of it.

Jonah double-checked his straps, tugged on the rope at his belt and felt for the leash connected to his ice ax. Now that he was facing this mountain with

Val by his side, he suddenly felt a need to be sure they would be safe. When it was just him, he hadn't cared all that much, but now he was responsible for her well-being, and he wasn't about to let her get hurt. Once he was positive everything was where it needed to be, he nodded to Val. "Ready. You?"

"Yep! Let's do this," she said, taking a step as if she couldn't wait another moment to try her hand at this challenge. The backpack that must've held forty pounds of equipment didn't seem to weigh her down. And he couldn't imagine her getting too tired and wondering if a helicopter might need to come get her from the side of *this* mountain. He smiled a little at that memory.

They walked carefully together through the murky darkness toward the first of the two glaciers they would need to traverse on their hike. The views from this altitude were spectacular, Jonah knew, but wouldn't be visible for hours. Still, it was much better to start early and get back down the mountain before the August sun had a chance to make the ice and snow even more treacherous. This mountain was dangerous enough without adding partially melted snow into the mix. Even with his knowledge and skills, he wouldn't be able to predict where crevasses might open up in the heat. Val seemed to understand that thinking, because she seemed very ready to begin her hike despite the early hour.

Jonah glanced at the woman walking beside him. She knew what she was getting into, right? He was overwhelmed by her change, but he couldn't see that and just assume she was truly prepared for Rainier. As confident as she seemed, this hike was more than a little strenuous, and it could be downright dangerous. If she wasn't actually ready, they very well might need to turn back before the summit. After all, half of all attempts failed—he knew that as well as anyone. And turning back wasn't the worst thing that could happen. How prepared was she, really?

"So, I never expected to see you on Mt. Rainier," Jonah began, his voice sounding loud compared to the soft crunching sound of their crampons on the ice.

Val chuckled. "Up until a year ago, I didn't expect to ever be up here. I've changed a lot since you first met me," she told him.

That much was obvious. "I believe you, but are you sure you're ready for this?" he asked, a little quieter this time. He gestured out at the expanse before them. Even in the dim moonlight and the tiny light from their headlamps, the mountain loomed dangerously ahead.

Her nod was as full of confidence as they came.

"I've summited Mt. Si several more times including a few times carrying up to sixty pounds of gear. I've been training on Mailbox Peak, taken survival classes and courses on mountaineering. I've been preparing for this day for months. I'm as ready as I'll ever be," she told him.

He couldn't help but grin at her list of accomplishments. It did sound like she'd taken this very seriously. The likelihood of her being too tired to go on after a couple thousand feet dropped significantly in his mind. She'd been busy over the past year, that was for sure. "Last we talked, I thought you'd never go up a mountain again," he said. "What made you decide to go the mountaineering route instead?"

After a brief pause, she gave an answer that surprised him enough to make him stop walking and just look at her.

"Meeting you," she said.

"Me?" he responded, sounding shocked. She noticed his footsteps stop.

Val turned toward him and laughed a little at how surprised he was at this news, shaking her head. She couldn't help it. He obviously had no idea what he'd done for her that day. "Yep, you. When you helped me get up Mt. Si, you showed me that my body was stronger than I believed. Your enthusiasm for being a mountain hiker and what you shared about the beautiful places around here—and Mt. Rainier in particular—stayed with me. I wanted to have those experiences myself."

She paused. There was so much more than just that, but she didn't know exactly what to say. How much she'd regretted not getting his number, and how she had looked for him during each hike she'd completed, hoping to see him again. How she was changed, body and soul, because of their few hours together. "I thank God every day for setting you on that mountain when I needed you," she finally said into the silence.

Jonah made a noise in his throat that made her turn toward him, but it was too dark to see his expression very well and she didn't want to shine her headlamp in his face to try to figure it out. "What are you thinking, Jonah?" she asked.

She could feel more than see his shrug. "I thought the exact same words you said to me back then. God hasn't done much for me lately. It's pretty funny, in a way."

He didn't sound like he thought it was funny at all. He sounded like he was angry, at himself or the world or God or all three, and she felt her heart ache for him. What could have possibly happened for someone who believed as strongly as he had to lose so much of his faith?

She didn't know yet, but she knew she was on the mountain with him because of his loss of faith and his pain and his anger. He needed somebody right then, and she would be that for him in any way she could. "You helped me reconnect with God, too. After meeting someone like you and learning what good can come from a difficult situation, I realized that He had been with me all along," she said.

She reached out and touched Jonah's arm, but he didn't respond to the gesture or words, or even look in her direction. He just kept walking at that same steady pace, and after a moment she let her hand drop to her side.

Please, Lord, let me help him.

His situation wasn't one where it was possible to find the good. Thinking about what God had allowed to happen made Jonah's chest hurt. He could hardly breathe, but it had nothing to do with the altitude and everything to do with the grief that was crashing over him like a wave, weighing him down and making every step a chore.

He'd gotten accustomed to it by now, though. He'd lived with it for the past two months and had become resigned to the constant pain. It no longer overwhelmed him the way it had at first; he'd learned to keep moving despite it.

That was all he could do—just keep moving. If he stopped and let himself think about Becca…

Well, he knew not to do that. He wasn't just sad anymore. He was angry, too, and thinking too much made the anger difficult to control.

So instead he tried to focus on the terrain in front of him, or at least what he could see of it in the moonlight and the glow of his headlamp. He listened to his footsteps making crunching sounds as they traversed the first of the glaciers they needed to cross to reach the peak. These were the things to think about, not his loss or what God had done. Val's footsteps crunched right along with his. He focused some of his attention back to her.

He still couldn't believe she had changed so much because of one afternoon on a mountain with him. That version of himself *had* been enthusiastic about hiking. And God. And lots of things. Now he could only look back at it as if that was another person entirely. He knew the change in him wasn't good, but how could it be any different when he'd been through such a loss?

He caught himself before the anger and sadness could crash over him entirely and tried to clear his mind before it bit into him again. It did no good to wallow—he had learned that—and he groped for something else to think about.

"Do you mind if I chatter while we walk?" Val asked, breaking the silence around them.

"Please chatter," he told her, wondering if she'd somehow known some of what he'd just been thinking. Or possibly she just didn't like the silence. Either way, he was thankful for it and eagerly listened as she started speaking.

"So my first time up the old trail to Mailbox Peak was ridiculous. It had rained the night before and the trail was such a mess. It took me hours, and by the time I got back down I was covered head to toe in mud. I was digging dirt out of all sorts of places for *weeks*."

Jonah chuckled, and the pressure on his heart eased for just a moment. Val continued telling him about her exploits and mishaps as she had prepared for this day, and he again marveled at the woman beside him.

Val wasn't an entirely different person from who she had been back when they first met, just less broken, more confident and happier. She still had that whatever-it-was that had captured his attention on Mt. Si all those months ago. Her humor, her sparkle, had all been there before, but the layer of hopelessness that had dulled them was gone and they shone out so brightly it took his breath away. She had told him on that day that she used to be chipper, and now he saw that she'd gotten that part of herself back.

They continued across the glacier, one step at a time, and Val talked while he listened. When she finished telling him about her hikes, there were more questions he had waiting.

"So obviously you're still living here. What happened with the job search?" he asked.

Her excitement immediately showed. "Oh yeah, I haven't told you about that!" she said.

He smiled at her enthusiasm and listened, waiting. "On one of my first hikes after Mt. Si, I met a really nice guy, and he just happened to be a writer. He introduced me to his editor and one thing led to another and I got a job just outside of Seattle. It's everything I hoped for." She was practically gushing.

She quieted down quickly, though, and seemed a little sad. He wasn't exactly sure why—perhaps it had to do with that guy she mentioned. He wanted to ask about it but decided not to. Her love life wasn't his concern. He'd wished it would be at various times over the past year, but now definitely wasn't the time for any of that.

In the silence, he noticed that she was breathing heavier than before. Of course she was: she'd been hiking hard for a long while now with a heavy pack and had been talking the entire time. Jonah didn't want to push her too hard and make this hike miserable for her. They had plenty of time to take breaks if she needed them. "Should we stop for a short rest?" he asked, slowing his pace to almost a stop.

But she kept going at the same speed and pulled ahead of him, forcing him to rush to catch up to her. "No way. We're not even halfway to Cathedral Gap yet. We just got started! You can't possibly be tired yet," she said with a little shake of her head.

He chuckled and matched her stride as they continued up the mountain. So there would be no taking it easy on her, that much was clear. He reminded himself that this version of Val was ready for the hike ahead as they continued along by the light of their headlamps.

They moved at a steady pace for a few more minutes while Jonah wondered about the dark, determined figure beside him. The fact that her breathing was just a little ragged and not gasps for air despite the lack of oxygen this high up was a testament to her training and fitness. He'd seen plenty of climbers give up without even stepping foot out of Camp Muir because they couldn't handle the altitude and knew it would only get worse on the ascent. But Val appeared undaunted, which seemed to be how she was approaching the world now, so differently than she had a year ago.

He wanted to ask about The Breakup—even just the little she had said about it back on Mt. Si had been enough to give it capital letters in his head—but he didn't want to poke at that wound. Even if it had been over a year old and she seemed to be in a much better place than she was back then, that didn't mean it was no longer a sore subject. Her fiancé had left her for somebody else, and that wasn't something you got over very easily, he was sure. Even if she was no longer broken, she could still be scarred.

He couldn't help but be curious, though. She'd been so hurt by what had happened between her and whatever-his-name-was that it had broken Jonah's heart to hear the pain in her voice when she'd mentioned it. She'd managed to hold herself together, but it was obvious she was struggling and lost. He remembered her expression when she'd told him about it, when she'd said God hadn't been on her side. His memories of that day still stood out sharply in his mind, but that was probably because he'd thought back over them so many times since that day.

He had been more than a little interested in Val. Everything about her fascinated him, from the way she half smiled even with tears in her eyes to her frank honesty about herself to the exasperated way she shoved her mass of tight curls out of her face. Even when crushed under sadness and loss, she had shone brighter than anyone he'd ever met. And she could make him laugh even when she was clearly struggling. He'd never met anybody like her.

He'd thought about her so much in the weeks and months after they'd met, wondering how she was doing, wishing he could see her again. He'd even avoided Mt. Si over the past year because it reminded him of her, and he knew it wouldn't be any fun to hike it without her by his side.

And now here she was, when romance was the furthest possible thing from his mind. This time *he* was the one so broken and crushed and hopeless that starting to date was simply impossible. They had switched places, leaving the problem the same as it had been before.

He shook his head and chuckled at the irony of it all.

"Want to let me in on the joke?" Val said, startling him out of his thoughts. He couldn't see her face much in the darkness, but he was sure she was watching him out of the corner of her eye.

Jonah didn't know what to say. He couldn't even begin to explain what had been going on in his mind, but he couldn't straight-out lie, either. The number of things he couldn't say weighed heavy on his chest.

But he had to say something. "When we met last year—" he began, not sure where he was going to go from there.

Luckily Val saved him. She shook her own head and said, "I know, I was such a mess that day. After what happened with Brian, I was in a very bad place. You caught me at my lowest point."

There was silence for a minute. Then Jonah said, "I don't know about you, but I need a snack and some water."

He was a little relieved that she didn't argue, and they both stopped, took off their packs and pulled on warm jackets to protect them from the cold that was so much worse when they weren't moving. Jonah grabbed a protein bar and his water, and she did the same. He was grateful she joined him without protest. Even as a seasoned hiker, the thin air on the mountain made regular breaks necessary, and they needed to keep their bodies hydrated and consume enough calories if they were going to make it all the way to the summit.

While they rested, he waited, silent, wondering if she had anything else to say about what had occurred, or if she was finished with the subject. After some time and a protein bar, she spoke again. "I really have gotten over everything that happened, and I credit a lot of that to you, and God, of course. I truly know who I am, and I don't think I would have done that if Brian and I had gone through with the wedding. I hope he's happier now and his life is better because we separated. I know mine is," she said, her voice thoughtful.

"Is he still with…" Jonah paused, not remembering the name of the bridesmaid who Brian had fallen for.

"Annalise? I don't know. If he is, I hope they're happy together, but I haven't kept in touch. I'm over it, but that doesn't mean I'm having either of them over for brunch anytime soon."

That last bit made him smile. Val was funny, that was for sure. She'd made him smile more in their time so far that morning than he'd smiled in months.

She said, "I was so hurt by everything that had happened, but I eventually moved past it." She paused. "I hope you can move past whatever is hurting you, too," she added quietly, all the humor gone from her voice.

Jonah felt the grief wash through him again. His loss wasn't something to move past in the same way a broken engagement was. It would color the rest of his life—he was sure of that much—and it changed everything for the worse. She couldn't possibly understand what he was going through. For the rest of his life, part of his heart would be missing.

But he didn't want to say any of that. He just wanted to hike up the mountain. "Are you ready, or do you need a longer break?" he asked, guessing that the question would be enough to get them moving again without him needing to respond or explain anything.

He waited for her response, hoping she wouldn't push the subject further. For a moment he thought she might, but then she put her water and jacket away and nodded. "Ready when you are," she said, hoisting her backpack.

He did the same and forced his feet to get moving. That was the only way to survive, after all. Keep moving, focus on the present. Don't think too much. Staying distracted was key.

And, as if to help distract him and keep him from ruminating on what he was unable to change, the ground began to move beneath his feet.

Chapter Three

"Earthquake!" she shouted much too loudly as adren-aline shot through her. She dropped to the ground, dig-ging her ax into the ice and holding on to it, not looking at Jonah, but hoping he was doing the same. They were tied together, and her ax should hold them if neces-sary, but the more secure they both were, the better.

They weren't in a spot where avalanches were likely, but you never could tell what would occur or how big the earthquake might be, so it was better to be ready for anything.

She heard Jonah, just a second behind her. His ax bit into the snow a few inches from her as his body dropped next to hers. He held the ax with one hand, his other arm wrapped around her protectively.

They listened and felt, waiting to see what might happen next.

In a few seconds, it was over. The earthquake had been barely more than a tremor, something you would hardly notice down at sea level. Still, they both stayed frozen in position, listening for sounds that might indicate an avalanche or other dangers, because safety wasn't ever a sure thing this high up. When minutes had passed but nothing had happened and it seemed like nothing would, they finally sat and looked at one another. "Well, that was my first earthquake," she told him. "I hoped I'd experience one while I was up here. Being on an active volcano and all."

"Hopefully that'll be the most exciting thing that happens," he said. "It's dangerous up here."

"I know," she said. "That's why I didn't let you go it alone."

He looked chagrined, and she felt a little guilty for the poke. "Thanks for doing the firefighter protecting thing," she added. "If it'd gotten bigger and anything *had* fallen our way, you could have saved my life."

She didn't say anything about how safe she'd felt with him there, his arm around her. It was better not to. They couldn't get too close. She was there to help him with his pain and to hike a mountain—that was it. Nothing more than that. She knew what her limitations were.

He gave her a little nod to acknowledge her thanks. "I'm just glad we're both safe," he told her.

They stood up and brushed the snow off, then started hiking again. She felt like the moment was a little too comfortable, too intimate, and she knew it couldn't go in that direction. So she did the only thing she could think of to break it: share a few fun facts. "Did you know that there can be as many as five earthquakes a month up here? It's actually one of the most dangerous volcanoes in the world because it's due for an eruption pretty soon, geologically speaking," she said.

"Geologically speaking?" he asked.

"Yeah," she explained, "because geologists measure things in decades and centuries and millennia, not days or months or years."

"I see," he said. Val felt a bit silly and wondered if he thought she was a little crazy because of her random prattle, but at least she'd changed the tone of the moment to something much less sweet. "You really did prepare for this hike," he commented, sounding impressed.

So he didn't think she was crazy. That was nice. "Yep," she told him. "I did some research and everything. Even read a whole Wikipedia article on it," she finished, wondering if he might laugh at that. He had laughed so easily on Mt. Si, and she had thought about that laugh so many times in the past year.

There was no laugh, but a slight chuckle did pass

his lips and she took that as good enough for now. A few seconds later, however, he was quiet and seemed burdened again by whatever relentless hurt had taken possession of his mind and heart since she'd seen him last.

Val watched Jonah's dark figure for an extra moment, absorbing the change in him, before turning her attention back to the snow and ice she was walking upon. She knew how important it was to keep her attention on her feet while she was out on the glacier. An injury would mean no summit. But half her mind was on the man walking slightly ahead of her, with that pained determination written on his face. She couldn't see it, but she could sense it in every line of his body.

Briefly as they hiked, it seemed like the terrible weight he was carrying lifted a little and allowed a smile or small chuckle to escape, but then it invariably came back full force minutes later. She wondered how long he'd been carrying it and if he got any real breaks, more than a few seconds here and there, from the hurt that seemed to have taken over his very person. It didn't seem likely, except perhaps when he was sleeping. Or possibly putting himself in danger.

She understood a little more why he might have been prepared to attempt this hike all on his own.

What had happened to him in the past year that had affected him so much? It was more than clear that he wasn't interested in talking about it, but she still wanted to help. The change in him saddened her.

The image of that strong man full of kindness and optimism who had sat down beside her on Mt. Si and offered her a granola bar, content to walk slowly with her as she struggled even though she was a complete stranger, came to her mind. He had been such a significant force in her life since then, although they hadn't seen each other again until their random meeting at Camp Muir that morning.

She wondered how she could be that kind of a force for him now, in his own time of need. She wasn't sure what the best plan of action was, and she prayed to God. Perhaps He would guide her.

"Almost at Cathedral Gap," Jonah told her, his voice cutting into her thoughts.

Val looked away from her feet for a moment and her headlamp shone on the scene ahead. In its light and the light of the moon, she could see where the reflective ice of the glacier ended and the mountain faded to black rock.

They were nearly done with the glacier, and she mentally checked it off as the first leg of the day's journey. Then she did a body scan to see how she was handling the hike. It was important not to ignore her body's signals out here, and she felt for signs of fatigue, blisters or strain. It was a relief to find that she was still feeling strong and her lungs were handling the thin air well. Her body was meeting this challenge like she had hoped it would.

The hike was going to get much more difficult, Val knew, but she could do this. She *needed* to do this. And she had already come this far without a problem. Just a few more hours and she would be at the tippy-top, she thought with a smile and a glance at Jonah—which killed the happy thought, because looking at him reminded her of how much he was hurting, though she didn't know why.

Soon, as they made their way through Cathedral Gap and tried to keep up their pace against the difficult elevation change, it would become hard to talk much, and she felt called to say something now, before it was too late. She wasn't sure if it was God or her own brain that told her to say something, but either one was enough to convince her to take that opportunity while she still had it. There was no time like the present.

"So, my grandma," she began, only realizing it was a rather abrupt topic introduction by his reaction. He jerked his head around so his headlamp was trained on her, and though she couldn't see him, she could practically feel the raised eyebrows he was giving her. She hoped he couldn't see her flushed cheeks in the harsh lamplight. But she had already jumped in and wasn't about to give up now. "I'm going somewhere with this, I promise," she reassured him with an encouraging nod. "My grandma had a copy of the Serenity Prayer up on her wall in the kitchen. Why it was in her kitchen, I don't know. She wasn't that great of a cook, so maybe it was there to remind her not to get too upset when the smoke alarm went off again," she joked.

It was too dark to tell if her attempt at humor had worked, but there was no laugh, so after a quick beat, she continued. "Anyway, every time I was there, I would read the words. You know, 'God, grant me the serenity to accept the things I cannot change, the courage to change the things I can, and the wisdom to know the difference.'"

She paused again, but he still made no comment, so she pressed on. "I've probably read those words a thousand times. They've become a part of my soul. Sometimes I forget them for a little while, but I always come back to the words, and they've helped me during my most difficult times."

Val thought about a day not so long ago, when she had been sitting in a specialist's office, staring at a beige wall covered in framed degrees while the words *cancer* and *chemotherapy* and *survival rates* washed over her. She had grasped that prayer like a life preserver as she started to drown under them and had felt a level of peace she hadn't expected even after all the times she had leaned on those words. She'd truly felt that God was with her then, and calmness had rushed through her.

She wasn't sure how she would have gotten through that moment without it.

Val took a second and brought herself away from the doctor's office and back into the present, where it was Jonah's problem that mattered. "I'm just saying, it's something to think about."

He gave a nod, but nothing more, and she thought he might be angry with her. They continued walking in silence. She didn't know if Jonah would take anything she said to heart or if she had just ruined the rest of their hike.

Cathedral Gap loomed directly in front of them, and she felt a sense of urgency to continue this conversation now, even if it was uncomfortable and even if Jonah would be unhappy with her. The easiest part of the hike was nearly over, and any chance to really talk was rapidly dwindling. Between the altitude and the effort required for the next few legs, deep conversation would be difficult if not impossible.

She needed to know what was going on with him if she had any hope of making that last little bit of conversation meaningful, and her time was running out to do so. Even though she didn't want to hurt him by making him talk about something he wasn't interested in discussing, she knew from personal experience that not talking about your problems didn't make them go away and often just made them worse. She made herself ask the hard question. "What happened this year, Jonah?"

She watched him, not sure what kind of answer she might receive. His jaw clenched and his movements became stiff, as if his body was tensing up for a fight. She thought he might not say anything at all, and that question would hang between them for the next few hours until they said goodbye back at Camp Muir. If he didn't answer, she wouldn't push again. She couldn't force him to talk, even if she hoped he would.

In the glow of his headlamp, she could see his jaw work, as if he was trying to relax the tension enough to open his mouth, as if he was trying to gain control of himself before speaking. Finally, he spoke. "Becca died," he said, sounding as if he was choking on the words.

Val heard the pain and grief in his voice and wondered if he'd ever actually said those words aloud. For a moment Val didn't remember who exactly Becca was. It had been a year ago when they'd talked, and some of the conversation had faded in that time. Then she realized who he was talking about and clutched at the chest of her jacket, feeling her heart ache for him. Jonah had told her about his twin sister, who asked for pictures from the tops of mountains.

They had been close, had shared that special connection twins sometimes did. It was clear from the way he talked about her that she was more than a sister, more than a friend. More like a part of who he was. And now she was gone, leaving Jonah behind.

"How long ago?"

"Ten weeks."

It felt like a physical blow to her gut. No wonder he was so broken. She remembered when her parents had died, so suddenly and unexpectedly, and what it had done to her. There were no words for that kind of pain or the struggle it took to get back to living again.

They had stopped walking, but Val was so lost in thought she'd hardly noticed the change. She was still trying to absorb the new information.

"Ready for the next big part of the hike?" he asked her, gesturing toward the wall of rocks in front of them. "You did good work on the glacier," he added.

Val looked at him for a long moment before focusing on Cathedral Gap, the second stage of their journey to the summit. It was clear he was changing the subject, but she didn't fight it for now and just tried to wrap her mind around everything going on.

They had made it this far and it was time for the next step. In other circumstances, she would have been awed by the outcroppings and excited about the completion of one part of the challenge, but her mind was still on Jonah and his sister.

She wanted to say something to him, offer him something to ease his pain, but what could she say? I know how you feel? I'm sorry for your loss? Nothing would help—nothing would be able to express the magnitude of her feelings or his, and it felt paltry to even attempt it.

And from the set expression on his face, it was clear he didn't want any words at the moment, even if she could manage to find some good ones. He just wanted to climb this mountain.

After staring at him for a few seconds, trying to decide what to do, she said the only thing she could think of: "Let's do it."

He nodded, looking more than a little relieved, and together they began to walk once again, going slower as they fought the steep incline of the gap that was the best way up and over the rocks. Climbing the rocks themselves would be shorter but more dangerous, and going around would send them out onto another glacier, which would be safer and easier at another time of year but full of hidden crevasses this late in the summer. So they tramped through the snowy gap, pushing their bodies up one step at a time.

Val made sure her pack was firmly on her back and focused her attention on what they were doing. She forced her thoughts to settle and stay in the here and now so she could safely accomplish the task at hand. There would be plenty of time to think about their conversation later. Right now safety was paramount, and being distracted wouldn't help her or Jonah.

Jonah breathed a sigh of relief when Val didn't push the topic any further, though he doubted the conversation was over just like that. He hoped she understood that he didn't want to talk about it. Even just managing those few words had been almost more than he could handle, and he was so tired of everyone trying to "fix" his pain. Like it was something that could just go away if enough people were sorry for his loss. He didn't want people's apologies—he just wanted his sister back in his life. He trudged on, hardly noticing his surroundings as thoughts of his twin threatened to bury him.

Ten weeks and two days ago, Becca was alive. She'd called him, even, to tell him about the ridiculous date she'd gone on. She had laughed until she was crying as she attempted to recount it for him. Ten weeks and one day ago, his phone rang again, but that call hadn't been from her, and there was no laughter on the other end. That phone call had changed his entire life, changed who he was. He'd been a pastor, a firefighter and a twin. Now what was he?

Jonah's boot slipped as he stepped onto an awkwardly jutting rock. He staggered for a second as he tried to regain his balance and fell to one knee, banging it painfully against the ground. His breath hissed between his teeth as he slipped off his pack and turned his light toward the knee, shifting his leg and stretching it out. He prodded it carefully with his fingers to see if there was any serious damage. If it was sprained or injured in any way, he'd need to call off the rest of the hike, and the thought of telling Val they were done was more than he could bear to imagine. All because of a stupid one-second mistake.

Luckily, it wasn't more than bruised. It hurt a little, but he was fine.

Val caught up to him. She must have fallen behind as he'd walked unthinkingly through the Gap. "Is it injured?" she asked, showing only concern for his welfare.

The look on her face made it clear she would be

nothing but kind if he'd actually gotten hurt and they needed to stop, no matter how much she wanted to finish the hike. She wouldn't blame him at all, even if it had happened because of his poor choices.

"It's fine, just a bruise," he told her, glad for the both of them that that's all it was.

She looked relieved. "I'm glad you're okay," she told him, sitting in the snow beside him for a brief rest.

Jonah was frustrated with himself. Up on the mountain, focus was more than important—it could mean the difference between a successful summit and going home all in one piece or being medevaced to the nearest hospital. Or worse. Between the experience of a lifetime and becoming a cautionary tale.

They stood back up and put their backpacks on. He put weight on his knee and was relieved to see that it was holding his weight just fine. Then he trained his eyes on what was in front of him, refocusing his headlamp's light on the ground and pushing the thoughts about his sister out of his mind.

That was why he was up on this mountain, after all. When he was at home, knowing he'd never get a silly emoji-filled text from his twin, he would start to feel like he couldn't breathe and the walls were closing in. Pushing himself to the limit of his endurance, needing to focus on every footstep and hand grab, were the only things that helped.

And not being able to breathe because he was twelve thousand feet above sea level was better than not being able to breathe because the world had fallen apart.

He straightened up, trained his eyes on the steep incline and dark rocks in front of him, and continued the steep hike, plus a little rock scrambling, up to Ingraham Flats, which would be a good place to get a decent rest. He listened carefully to Val's breathing and her footsteps. With the lead rope tying them together, any loss of attention was dangerous for her as well, because she was his last line of safety if something went wrong. If a tumble caught her unawares, they could be dragged down the mountain together.

When he was alone, having an accident on the mountain didn't worry him and he was willing to do some risky things. In fact, he'd done quite a few of them in the past ten weeks. But he wasn't alone and Val mattered; she was depending on him to keep them both safe, and he didn't want to put her in danger.

Not that she seemed in any danger of being caught with her attention wandering at a crucial moment, even if he was. She had reacted instantly to the earthquake earlier, taking the exact right safety precautions like she'd done it a thousand times. And now, here in the Gap, he could see that every movement she made was deliberate and careful. She wasn't going to be surprised by a loose rock or a shifting footstep or a partner who endangered himself by getting distracted when he should be focused on the terrain. Everything she did was like a carefully composed work of art.

He had to force himself to focus again, but for a very different reason. Val grabbed his attention in a way he'd never experienced before, and he silently berated himself for getting distracted by her. It was hard to look away. She had been lighthearted and funny as they'd crossed the glacier, but now, when the trail became difficult, she attacked it with a sincere earnestness that made him want to simply watch her. She was so calm, so intent on the task before her. He found himself staring at her more than he would like.

Because if he was too attracted to her, he might try to date her and drag her into his broken life, and she didn't deserve that. So he tore his eyes from her and continued on his way.

Val kept her eyes on her own feet, but she listened carefully to Jonah's movements. He seemed to have himself under control now and was carefully plodding along up the mountain. He paused for a few seconds and watched her but he didn't say anything, so she tried to assume he was waiting for her to catch up. Or perhaps he'd paused to wonder how she could be so awful as to remind him of the worst thing that had ever happened in his life.

She could kick herself for bringing up his sister's death when he was clearly up here to forget about it. He'd been planning to do this dangerous hike alone because he wanted to get away from his pain, and here she was, begging to go with him and then asking him about the most painful thing he'd ever experienced. Which had happened only a few weeks ago.

She prayed God would help her lighten his burden rather than make it any heavier for the rest of the hike.

She knew how unmooring it felt to lose people you loved, and how sometimes running from the pain felt like the best option. She knew it more than most. And she couldn't blame Jonah for wanting to lose himself in the physical exhaustion of hiking this mountain. She just hoped it was only that, not a desire to put himself in a dangerous situation. He wouldn't be the first person to risk his life when confronted with loss.

Val scrambled over a rock face, finding small hand- and footholds to help her up it, her crampons scraping along. She was a little behind Jonah, following his path as they made their way through the last bit of the Gap. It reminded her of the haystack at the top of Mt. Si, which had been her first experience scrambling up anything since she was a kid. This time she was carrying forty pounds on her back, but she was so much stronger and more competent than she'd been then.

Still, she could feel her breath becoming ragged. Her legs were burning, and she was dying for a few minutes to rest and eat something to boost her energy, but she gritted her teeth and dug her crampons into the icy snow as she searched for a handhold to use to pull her body up and over a section of rock. Now was the time to push through, get to the flat section on the other side where they could truly rest with a smaller danger of an avalanche or a fall. She'd studied everything well enough to know that The Flats was a relatively safe area, and they were almost there.

And she could do this. She had no doubt about that. Her gloved hand gripped the lip of rock and she hauled her weight up enough for her to find a spot for her foot. Another reach and another foothold and she was at the top of that small section, taking deep breaths as she got to her feet. Just a few more rock faces to scramble and they would be there, with one more section under their belts on the way to the summit.

They were making good time, and even though she wanted to rest for a few minutes, she knew she still had plenty left in her. Which she would need in order to get to the top. As she and Jonah reached the next rock face, she studied it and shook out her muscles in preparation.

"Coming down!" a voice called out from above, startling Val.

She looked up, surprised to see several headlamps trained on her. Then she realized it was the group she had seen leaving Camp Muir a few minutes ahead of her and Jonah.

The two of them stepped aside, allowing the other hikers to make their way down. After a few minutes, the group landed in the snow below the boulder, along with some skittering pebbles they brought down with them.

"Sorry about that," a woman in the group said as she dusted off her pants and adjusted her pack. "Having a good hike so far?" she asked while the two groups shook hands all around.

Val nodded, curious what made them turn around so soon. "Not too bad. Everything alright with you guys?"

The woman shrugged. "My friend busted his elbow on one of the rocks, and a couple of us just aren't handling the thin air very well. With that storm moving in tomorrow, we decided it was better to give up for now and try again another day."

Val was impressed with the woman's casual manner about needing to give up and go home so quickly. "I hope everyone makes it down safely," she told them.

"Oh, we intend to. That's why we're stopping now," the woman explained. "I've attempted Rainier eleven times. Made it to the summit on three of them. There will be other, better days."

Val wished that was true for herself, too, but it wasn't something she could guarantee. Today was her day.

The woman crossed her arms. "You sure you want to try to hike it today? That weather system moving in looks pretty ugly."

Val glanced at Jonah, who gave her a look that told her to take the lead on that one. "Thanks, but we're going to give it a shot," she said.

The other woman nodded. They said their goodbyes, and then the two groups parted. Val looked at the rock in front of her again and found her first handhold. She smiled a little to herself. She was actually doing this. She *could* actually do this.

When Jonah reached the top of the final rock face, he turned and waited for Val, a hand extended down to pull her over the last lip of Cathedral Gap that heralded Ingraham Flats, the next part of their journey.

Val looked up into his eyes and gave him her hand, along with a proud little smile, and he felt his heart miss a beat. His gloved fingers wrapped around hers, and in a moment she was sitting beside him, looking back into the darkness they had just traversed.

He couldn't believe how well Val had done on those rocks, pulling her body and her gear up and over without a single word of complaint, never stopping. She had sounded so confident when speaking to those other hikers. But now they were on The Flats and he could see that she was exhausted.

"Let's take a break," he said, knowing they both needed a long rest after all that exertion making it through the Gap if they planned to make it to the summit successfully. No rests and no food made you weak when you needed to keep pushing.

"We're making good time," she commented as she plopped down on the ground and began digging into her pack. "We should be back well before the sun starts melting everything."

He agreed. They hiked well together, keeping a steady pace that wasn't too fast or too slow for either of them. Part of him wanted to hike his next hike with her. Or the next hundred, perhaps. But he pushed aside that thought and set his mind to the necessary steps that needed to be done during breaks.

They pulled on their big coats and sat beside each other, looking out across the expanse of The Flats. It was time to rest, drink some water and down another couple granola and energy bars. Lack of calories on a hike this big could have dangerous outcomes, and they took advantage of the rest to replenish some of what they'd worked off. Val pulled off her helmet and messed with her hair, which fell around her shoulders in cascades of curls. Jonah caught himself staring and forced himself to turn away.

The silence between them felt heavy. He understood why. What was there to say after what he'd told her the last time they'd spoken? He wished he could come up with something easy to discuss, but he couldn't do more than watch her as she recuperated. His brain seemed to stutter to a halt every time she moved, and it took all his mental powers to chew his energy bar.

They locked eyes and he smiled. She smiled back and his heart felt lighter than it had in weeks.

Guilt rushed through him. Yes, he'd been attracted to Val when they'd met a year ago, but this wasn't the time to follow through with that attraction. He was too broken. Becca had *just* died.

It seemed they always met at just the wrong times.

Jonah turned away.

He started talking about the hike just to have something break the moment, although he was sure she knew everything already. "So we'll cross The Flats to Disappointment Cleaver and take that route, if that's okay with you. It's safer than going out on the glacier but we have to cross quickly because that overhang can send down rocks onto your head if you dillydally."

She chuckled and he looked at her, but she didn't explain the humor. "What was so funny?" he asked.

"No, nothing. No dillydallying. Got it."

He laughed and bumped her with his shoulder. "I can't help it. I was a youth pastor for a long time," he said. "I'm sure at some point today I'll remind you to stick with your buddy."

"*Was* a youth pastor?" Val prompted.

Jonah sobered. "Yeah. After…" He couldn't say it again so soon, so he just skipped the rest of that sentence. "I prayed a lot the first week. And it didn't get better, and I couldn't pray anymore. And I haven't since. I can't go back to being a youth pastor if I can't even pray."

There was a long silence while she seemed to digest this.

"You might want to try praying again. You need God now more than ever."

Jonah knew Val meant well, but he couldn't bite his tongue at that. "I've gotten that advice from plenty of people, but they don't know what it's like to lose somebody that close to you. It isn't that easy," he said, realizing how bitter he sounded without being able to do anything to stop it.

She didn't answer for a few seconds. When she did, her voice was calm and quiet. "I haven't lost a twin, but I've experienced loss, too," she told him.

"Your fiancé cheating on you isn't the same," he said, each word containing its own little bite at her lack of understanding.

The second the harsh words were out, though, he wished he could take them back. It was an awful thing to say and he knew it, and she was only trying to help. It was still dark, but he could see her well enough in the light of his headlamp to see her body crumple a little, as if she'd been punched in the gut, before she straightened up again. "I'm so sorry," he said, knowing that didn't make it better.

She looked him in the eye, and he could see the sorrow there. "I wasn't talking about that. My parents died in a car crash when I was in college," she said simply.

She didn't chastise him for what he'd said. Her tone met his bitterness and anger with compassion and calm, and guilt washed through him.

His heart stuttered as he processed her words. She had lost so much, so young. To be just starting her independent life and lose so much of her family all at once was incomprehensible. And yet here she was a few years later, strong and happy, with faith in God and prayer. Perhaps, if she could survive that kind of a loss, he could survive, too. "Oh," he said, almost before he realized he was speaking out loud.

She nodded. "Yeah. It was awful. I was twenty-one, and it felt like I was alone in the world. Brian and I had just started dating, and they had met him a few weeks before. They were so excited for me to have my first real boyfriend."

She paused for a second as if she was lost in thought, and he waited for whatever might come next, though he couldn't guess what it could be she was considering. "I think that's why I ignored all the signs that he didn't really care about me and was just in it because it was easy. I didn't want to give up that last connection I had with them, even so far as to get engaged," she said, sounding like she might have just realized that for the first time.

After a moment, she focused her attention back on him. "But I eventually lost that, too, and that was for the best. No matter what hard stuff comes your way, you have to keep going. The only other choice is to stop truly living your life, and that seems like no choice at all.

"I've chosen to keep going, and I've learned to accept that some things don't go the way we want. There have been low moments, of course, but I still have faith that God is there, and He has His reasons and is helping me through it all. Just like He's helped me today."

Jonah heard the husky note in her voice that indicated she was close to tears, and his heart went out to her. She made a little sniffling sound and then took another drink of water. When she spoke again, her voice was once again clear and strong. "So, from someone who's been through some tough times before, I suggest you keep trying to pray. It'll do you good."

Jonah looked away from her, out into the darkness. She truly was extraordinary. To go through all she had and to come out the other side of it with this attitude—it was amazing. And to be kind to him even when he lashed out at her, despite the fact that she was the person who deserved it the least… Extraordinary. He felt the twinge of guilt again.

"I really am sorry for what I said. I was wrong, but even if I hadn't been, I was still unkind when you were only trying to help."

She bumped him with her shoulder, just like he

had done to her a few minutes before, which made him smile. "You're lucky. I have to forgive you. After all, I still need you to get me up this mountain. I need to stick with my buddy," she said with a smile in her voice.

He chuckled. "I think you'd make it to the top just fine without me," he said, completely honest.

"Climb this thing alone? You'd have to be crazy to do something like that," she said with a little laugh, standing and stretching, seemingly ready to begin the hike once again.

He stood, too, not sure what to say to that. She had said it as a friendly tease, not being unkind, and he knew what she said was true, but he still couldn't come up with any response better than a shrug. He looked at her again, and even in the darkness he found himself lost in her jade eyes. His heart thumped painfully in his chest, but not in the unpleasant way it usually did. This was a feeling he wanted to feel again and again.

She was someone who seemed to go through all her life, even the hard parts, with a bit of good humor, he thought to himself. Jonah imagined for a brief second what a life with Val would be like, and he didn't even notice the little smile that thought brought to his face until Val looked at him as she unwrapped a candy bar and returned the smile. He felt the always-present tension in his body ease a little. For a second he wondered if she knew what he was thinking and considered telling her, but thought better of it. Really, it didn't matter *why* they were smiling. Just that they were there in that moment together.

Val looked away from him, shifting her body and breaking the spell, and he realized he'd been staring. He blinked and turned away, too, taking a deep breath of the thin air.

"So we should probably get going, if you're ready," he said, getting the conversation back on track.

"Let's show these Flats what we're made of," Val said. She put her helmet back on before settling her backpack into place.

Jonah almost grabbed Val's hand as it swung to her side. He was suddenly desperate to touch her again. Something more than the little shoulder bumps they had shared. The ease with which he could talk to her, the way she spoke—all honesty and kindness—made him want to hold her close and forget about the hike and the rest of the world.

But she had already turned to begin moving again, and he bit back those inclinations and kept his hands at his sides. He prepared his own gear and in a few minutes they were walking up the mountain once again, close but much farther apart than he wished.

As soon as they started again on their journey,

silence settled back between them, but it didn't feel heavy, like it needed to be broken. It was just there, a comfortable silence between two people who didn't need to speak to be with one another. They walked in it companionably.

Val walked beside Jonah, taking little glances at him out of the corner of her eye. She wasn't sure exactly what had been on his mind when he'd started smiling like that, but it made her heart swell to see him smile at all, so it didn't matter much what the reason was. She was sure he hadn't sent that many smiles out into the world over the past few weeks, and if anything could manage to break through that wall of pain, she thanked God for it.

Even though she was staring at the ground to watch for dangers, with only the occasional glance in his direction, Val could feel Jonah's presence beside her as they walked across the wide flat expanse. Their crampons crunched through the snow of The Flats, which despite their innocent name still managed to be a rigorous hike this high up.

They had hours left to hike, though they were moving at a steady pace and the summit felt so close she could almost touch it now that they were on the third big leg of the journey. Part of her wanted to slow everything down, give them more time. She felt like they had so much more to say and not nearly enough time or breath to say it.

But she didn't even know where to begin, and the silence wasn't tense or unpleasant, so she took a few breaths and let herself enjoy it as they walked side by side. The two of them traversed The Flats, crampons biting into the ice-crusted snow, still moving through the darkness with the setting moon and their headlamps the only light. Dawn was still an hour or two away, and hopefully by then they would be closing in on High Break and the last push to the summit.

More of the hikers had probably left Camp Muir to try their luck at a summit attempt that day, and the thought made Val a little sad. She knew it was silly, but for a while it felt as if they were the only ones out on this hike, the only two experiencing what it was like to climb through the darkness with hopes of writing their names in the book that waited at the peak for anyone who managed such a feat as summiting Mt. Rainier.

"I wonder how many are hiking today," she said, for no other reason than to share a little bit of her internal ponderings with him.

Jonah thought for a few seconds, then responded, "Probably not that many. Because of the storm coming in tomorrow, I imagine quite a few changed their plans for later in the week, to be on the safe side."

Val nodded. That hadn't been an option for her, or she probably would have done the same. And from what she knew of Jonah's journey thus far, safety didn't seem to have been at the forefront of his thoughts when he'd made the decision to hike today.

Val glanced at Jonah as silence settled in once again. On Mt. Si, even with the struggles of the mountain and her own woes, their conversation was constantly flowing, easy. Mostly because of Jonah's unflappable good humor. The quiet between them now wasn't bad, just different.

And she couldn't help but worry about Jonah. He seemed to only be able to be happy for a moment or two before dropping back into his grief. With something so recent and painful, that wasn't unexpected or anything but reasonable, and she didn't begrudge him his grief. It was too big to break through right now, and she had nothing but empathy for that. Still, she mourned the change and hoped it wouldn't be a permanent one, for his sake.

She also wished she could take the time to be with him and help as he dealt with all his hurt, but she knew that wasn't in the cards. She wouldn't be able to help like she wanted now and would only end up adding more to his burden, which was something she refused to do. Maybe she could reconnect with him after she finished chemotherapy, if everything went well.

The uncertainty there made her heart beat faster before she took a deep soothing breath and calmed it. She knew there was no reason to be afraid, whatever happened. God would give her the strength to accept it.

"We're coming up on some other hikers," Jonah said, breaking the silence.

Val lifted her eyes from the ground and looked ahead to see the light of three headlamps. They hadn't been the only ones on The Flats, it seemed, no matter how it had felt. A small group must have stayed there overnight to cut down on the length of their summit day. She envied their fresh legs and later wake-up time, but not another day spent breathing this thin air or carrying the heavier packs full of camping gear. There was always a trade-off.

In a few minutes she and Jonah had reached the small camp, where the group was working to stuff everything into their backpacks. The three hikers looked up at Val and Jonah and greeted them.

Val returned the greeting and paused to take a drink of water. The glow of all the headlamps made it feel like a relatively bright spot in the night. "You two start from Camp Muir?" one of the men asked her.

"Yeah. We started around midnight," she answered. She loved how friendly and helpful hikers tended to be out on the mountains, but right now it was difficult to muster the energy to engage in much chitchat.

He nodded, and he looked impressed. "You're making good time," he told her. "How's it been?"

That was a hard question to answer, so she just stuck to talking about the hike itself and using as few words as possible. "Mostly uneventful, except for a tiny earthquake a while back," she said.

She didn't even need to look at Jonah to know he had thoughts about her description. She could practically hear what he was thinking. The hike itself was pretty uneventful, sure, but it certainly hadn't felt like that for either of them.

"We must've all slept right through the earthquake," the man said. "But 'mostly uneventful' is good, don't you think? Or are you the kind of woman that likes a little extra excitement along the way?"

Val wasn't sure what to say to that. It gave her a distinctly uneasy feeling, though she couldn't pinpoint why. "Uneventful is good," she told him, putting her water away and preparing for her and Jonah to continue on their way.

"Even when it's uneventful, Mt. Rainier is a tough mountain, that's for sure," the man said, sounding like he'd done it so many times it wasn't actually tough for *him*. "I imagine most couples wouldn't attempt something like this together," he finished, gesturing to her and Jonah.

Val almost let it slide. She was done talking to him and, after all, what did it matter if he thought they were a couple?

But her heart liked that word a little too much, and a glance at Jonah told her he heard the word, too. And even though she couldn't quite read his expression, it was better to say the truth aloud. For both of them. "We're just friends," she said. "But we're doing great. I can't imagine a better hiking partner."

She hoped Jonah couldn't see the constrained edge to her smile as she said that. Her heart was protesting too hard for it to be fully genuine.

Everything she'd said was true, and the sooner she got that through her head, the better. They wouldn't be more than friends anytime soon, and fantasizing about it being anything else would just hurt more in the long run.

The man and Jonah were both looking at her. She couldn't bear to see what Jonah was thinking, so she kept her eyes on the stranger. She wanted to leave but didn't know how to break this awkward moment. The man stared at her, and Val started to feel a little uncomfortable under his gaze, though she couldn't quite explain why.

"Well, I'm sorry we missed out on the earthquake," he said, filling the silence.

Val felt a measure of relief to be on a better topic and hoped they would be wrapping up this conversation soon. She thought back to the earthquake, remembering the pressure of Jonah's arm around her, protecting her. It had been an interesting moment in more ways than one.

"They happen all the time up here. Mt. Rainier is an active volcano," he told her as if he was sharing little-known information.

Val nodded again, but she didn't have anything to say to that. There was a little empty silence and it seemed like a fine time to say goodbye. She opened her mouth to say exactly that.

"Have you ever hiked Rainier before?" he asked her before she got the chance.

She shifted gears quickly. Apparently they weren't leaving quite this second, but at least now she could bring Jonah more into the conversation and possibly fade into the background a bit. "No, but Jonah has," she said, turning toward him as she said it.

The man gave Jonah a brief glance before turning his attention back to her. "Well, congratulations for making it this far. You must be pretty tough to have made such good time and not be falling to pieces right now."

"Thanks," she answered. "Well, we should—"

"So your name is Jonah," he said, cutting her off and pointing to Jonah. "But what's your name?" he asked her.

"Val," she said, more than ready to wrap this up.

"Keith," he responded with a grin.

"Nice to meet you," she said. Then, before he could come up with something else to say, she added, "But we should really get back to it."

"Well, we're going to be ready in just a few minutes. How about you take a little break and then we could summit together?" Keith asked Val, giving her a winning smile.

Val paused for just a second to consider this idea before dismissing it entirely. A bigger group was certainly safer, but she wanted to get as far away from this Keith as she could. And...

And she wanted to spend this time with Jonah. Only Jonah. Even if they were just going to be friends, she wanted this time with him.

"What would you like to do, Val?" Jonah asked, his voice pulling her out of her thoughts.

She turned to him. The light was still very dim, but it was enough to see his expression, and this one she could read as clearly as if it were midday, and it agreed with her. She turned back to the campers. "I think we'll keep going. We had a long break not too long ago and want to keep moving. But maybe we'll see you out there."

The man looked to Jonah, as if he was waiting for him to overrule her, then returned his attention to Val. He shrugged and smiled at her again. "Well, we'll catch up if we can. Good luck out there," he told them. "Stay safe."

Val and Jonah waved goodbye and continued walking together, just the two of them. Val very much hoped that group would *not* catch up, and she set a pretty brisk pace to keep it from happening. She heard Jonah make an amused noise next to her and knew he saw exactly what she was doing, but he didn't protest and kept up, so she didn't slow down.

Val glanced over and Jonah caught her eye. "I just want to make up for lost time," she told him with a grin.

"Sure. Lost time," he agreed with humor in his eyes.

Val turned her attention back to her feet but couldn't stop smiling. She might have some hard times ahead, but she was going to summit this mountain with Jonah by her side, so it definitely wasn't all bad.

"That guy back there was not very happy you turned him down," Jonah told her once they had walked a little while.

"I wasn't very comfortable around him. Besides,

he has his friends. I don't think another two people would make a big difference in his experience, except giving him more people to talk to, I guess," she said.

"He would talk to you the whole way up and back if he was given half the chance," Jonah commented.

"I don't know why he attached himself to me like that," Val said. "I wasn't being all that friendly."

"It's pretty obvious why, isn't it?" Jonah asked, sounding a little incredulous.

Val thought through the conversation and couldn't come up with anything she'd said that was particularly interesting. "Not really," she said, feeling like she was being left out of a joke.

"He likes you, Val. I'm surprised he didn't ask you out on a date before we left," he said.

Val realized he was right as soon as she thought about it. "Oh wow, that wasn't going to go anywhere," she said.

"Yeah, you definitely didn't make it easy on him," he said with a laugh.

He didn't fully understand, though. With her diagnosis, she wanted to stay as far away from romance as she could. No sense in dragging someone else into the mess of cancer treatments and possible heartache if it didn't work. No, this was something she needed to do alone.

Even if none of that was true, though, she wouldn't have been going on any dates with Keith. Her interests lay…elsewhere. She sneaked a glance at Jonah. He was looking ahead, his expression thoughtful. Val wondered if he knew what she was thinking. It would be best to tell him she wasn't dating, make that extremely clear, but the words died in her throat. She'd say something if it came up, she promised herself.

"We're almost at Disappointment Cleaver," Jonah said to her. "You know the deal with this leg, right?"

"Yep," she answered. "A very short break before we tackle it?" she asked, looking back to ensure they wouldn't have company anytime soon.

"At this pace we'll leave Keith in the dust no problem, even with a break," Jonah said.

Val laughed. "You saw what I was doing there, huh?" she asked.

"You practically ran away from their little camp," he said. "I'm impressed with myself that I could keep up."

Val's heart jumped a little in her chest. He sounded like Jonah again. Even if it was only for a few seconds, the real him was still there, just waiting underneath the grief. It made her happy to know that. They locked eyes for just a moment.

Then she looked ahead and forced all of her attention on the terrain. This part of the hike wasn't easy;

it was as strenuous as the rest, only with an overhang that sometimes dropped bits and pieces down
onto the trail, or onto whoever was on the trail. And
sometimes those pieces were massive boulders. The
name of the game was to move fast. There would be
no breaks until they came out the other side.

Val dropped her bag and prepared for the long
haul ahead. A snack, some water. For some reason,
she didn't want to look at Jonah. All that talk of Keith
and thinking about dating just reminded her that
things with him would be going nowhere, and that
was hard to accept sometimes when she looked into
those warm eyes. Better to look elsewhere, push it all
out of her mind and keep her attention on the hike.

Disappointment Cleaver was safer than going out
on the glacier and risking falling into one of the
many hidden crevasses likely to be there this time
of year, but that didn't mean the Cleaver was *safe*.
This was not the time to be distracted.

And, she realized, it had started to snow.

Jonah seemed to notice at the same time, and he
put out his gloved hand. They both watched a few
flakes settle on it.

Even though it was August, snow could happen
up here any time of the year, and the flakes drift-
ing from the sky weren't a complete surprise. She

was, after all, surrounded by snow and had been all morning. Still, it was beautiful.

It was also potentially dangerous if it got too bad. She was grateful she had spare clothing in her bag in case she got wet from the snow as it melted on her. The air was freezing this high up, and being wet could spell disaster.

Val took a final drink of water, closed up her backpack and settled it back on her shoulders, shifting it into place and checking all the buckles to be sure it would be comfortable during this push. Jonah did the same.

"The overhang might keep the snow off, at least," he said as they prepared to continue.

"Perfect timing," Val said with a smile. Then she took as deep a breath as she could, the icy air entering her lungs as a few flakes landed on her lips. "Ready to get started?" she asked.

"Ready," Jonah responded.

Chapter Four

They kept a quick pace along Disappointment Cleaver. The rocks that perched precariously over their heads appeared as darker outlines against an only slightly lighter sky. Dawn came early at this time of year, but it would still be a while before the sun would make its debut. Not that they would see it when it did, with the clouds surrounding them and snow coming down. It was possible this weather would disappear in a few minutes, or they might hike high enough to get above the clouds and then might manage to see a sunrise, but the chance of either of those happening was slim.

Even with no sunrise to look forward to and a little snow coming down, Jonah was feeling good about their hike. They were making good time, as that guy Keith had noted. Jonah had to smirk at the man's very obvious attempt to flirt with Val and her complete lack of interest in him. He knew he himself was too broken to be dating anyone right now, but it still sent a spark of hope straight to his heart.

She didn't want to hike with anyone but him, and she had zero interest in Keith. So maybe...

Jonah felt guilt rush through him. He was in *mourning*. This wasn't the time to start thinking about romance. And besides, Val had very pointedly called them friends. She was right—that's all they were and all they could be.

He put his mind back on the hike, mentally reviewing the final steps to the summit. He knew there were some rough spots ahead, especially that final push when the air was so thin and you were so tired that every step felt like a challenge, but if the hike so far was any indication, Val would handle it just fine. It seemed like this would be a relatively easy summit, and he couldn't wait to see her excitement when they reached the top.

As if in response to his optimism, the snow began falling harder and the wind picked up, causing the flakes to swirl around them. He hoped it would go back to just a light dusting and then peter out, or this could be trouble.

He must've slowed his pace or Val sped up, because suddenly she was right behind him. "Let's pray this doesn't get any worse," she said in his ear.

Jonah nodded, though he couldn't actually pray, despite her earlier advice. He was so out of practice, and snow seemed like such a small prayer when there were so many other things to ask for. But he could hear her murmuring and felt sure she was sending a prayer up to God for the both of them. Even though he wanted to think it was silly, he felt a little better.

The overhang still kept most of the snow off them, but the wind was definitely picking up and occasionally the little flecks caught them in the face. It seemed pretty steady and wasn't getting worse, though, and Jonah wondered if Val's prayers were being answered.

After a few more minutes of walking, however, the snow started falling harder, and his hopes dwindled. He began to fear that it was going to be much, much worse than a short burst of flakes. The wind picked up, blowing the snow into his eyes, making him blink and wipe them in an attempt to clear them enough to see. No, this wasn't good at all.

And then the flakes started to drop hard and fast, and fat heavy flakes surrounded them, making the world disappear. The overhang was a little protection but not much. Not enough. The snow blew into his face again, with enough force to make him sputter.

He stopped walking and turned toward Val, who'd been walking close behind him and had been shielded a little from the blast.

"Jonah?" Val said, resting a hand on his shoulder. "We should keep going, right? Get out from the overhang?"

He could see her staring hopefully into his face, but everything else around them was a mass of white as the snow dumped down, occasionally swirling against them with the gusts of wind. They were officially in a whiteout now, and he ran through their options, trying to decide what would be best. With visibility down to nothing, the chances of getting lost or hurt skyrocketed. It was best to hunker down and wait for the weather to improve, but doing so here, under the rocks, presented its own dangers. She knew all that as well as he did; he could see it in her eyes. There was also trust there, as if she had absolute confidence in his ability to make the right decision and get them out of this safely.

He looked around at where they were, at the rocks overhead. They would get weighed down with heavy accumulating snow, and falling boulders would become more and more likely. They couldn't stay where they were and risk one coming down on them, but the whiteout wasn't safe to hike in, either, and if they went out onto the glacier here, they wouldn't even be able to see the most obvious of the crevasses and could easily lose sight of the trail. Wandering away from the overhang without any concept of where they were was not an acceptable choice in conditions like this.

People died in just this situation every couple of years. A surprise whiteout led to hypothermia, injuries or death if hikers weren't incredibly careful. They had to get safe, and they had to do it quickly. Val's life was at risk, and he would do anything he could to keep her safe. He made a decision and leaned close so she could hear him clearly.

"Stay close behind me. Keep your fingers touching the wall. We're going to get out of here fast," he told her, looking into her eyes for understanding.

She nodded and put her hand on the rocks, ready to follow his lead. It was clear she understood the danger, and that she was ready to do whatever was necessary, and she had the energy and strength to do what needed to be done. And he could see that she trusted him to keep her safe. Well, him and God.

Jonah sure hoped He was there with them on this mountain, because they could use all the help they could get. Jonah turned and felt Val's other hand settle onto his shoulder. She squeezed to let him know she was ready, then left it there. It was a normal thing to do in a whiteout, keeping a hand on the lead hiker in order to keep each other close and safe, but it felt like much more than that. He felt its weight there, solid and sure in him and in God. He felt a sense of calm wash over him.

They started walking again, making their way as swiftly as they safely could. Jonah didn't want to push too hard and wear either of them out, but it was best to move at a faster pace than he'd otherwise set. And although Jonah worried about Val being able to keep up and was ready to slow down the moment she needed him to, her hand never slipped from its place on his shoulder.

Inhaling was painful, each breath full of too-thin air and cold snow, but he ignored it. He would get her somewhere safe. That propelled him forward each step.

Then Jonah heard the loud crack of a boulder peeling off the cliff face somewhere high above them, along with the skittering tumble of smaller rocks the large one brought down with it. His footsteps hesitated, but he didn't allow himself to pause as he listened for the rocks to fall, wondering where it all would land. Val squeezed his shoulder, and he could feel her tense up behind him as she waited, too, but she kept pace with him. *God, please help us through this*, he thought involuntarily.

After what felt like much too long, he heard the

wet thump as everything crashed down somewhere behind them. Relief flooded through him and he took a calming breath. They were still unharmed, though how many more boulders might come crashing down with this weather was anybody's guess, and he didn't want to wait around and find out.

It was impossible to tell how much farther they had left with the view ahead completely hidden by falling snow. But it couldn't be very long before they would be past the overhang, which meant they'd be more exposed to the wind but would no longer need to worry about rocks falling on their heads. He'd take that trade any day of the week.

There was another loud crack, another moment of listening and hoping for the reassuring thump in the distance, and then the crash as a boulder hit other rocks and finally settled in the snow. Close, but not close enough to injure them. They continued moving as quickly as they reasonably could at this altitude with snow blowing in their faces.

Jonah listened intently for the next crack, but there was nothing except the sound of the wind and the snow that surrounded them. His attention shifted to his gloved hand still touching the wall of rock, then to Val's hand on his shoulder. They were still there, still on the right track, still safe. He bent his head and plowed forward, hardly noticing the cold. His only thought was that he needed to get Val safe. She trusted him and he wouldn't let her down.

Then the small amount of coverage they had from the rocks overhead disappeared, leaving the snow driving down heavily on them both. It was colder and wetter and windier than a few moments before, but Jonah was ecstatic because it meant they were out of Disappointment Cleaver. Not safe, exactly, but away from one big danger. He felt some of his worry lift. Val squeezed his shoulder again, and he knew that she felt the same way.

They walked just a little farther, and then Jonah stopped. He breathed a sigh of relief. They weren't protected from the weather, but at least boulders wouldn't come down on their heads out here.

As if in response, there was a crash of another section of rocks tumbling down, with a loud and heavy thump as it settled farther down the mountain. Even though Jonah hadn't liked Keith all that much, he certainly didn't want him to get crushed by falling rocks and hoped the three hikers were still on The Flats, away from Disappointment Cleaver and the glacier, sheltering safely from the storm.

Which is what he and Val needed to do now that they were out from the overhang and getting battered by the wind and snowfall. The gusts howled around them, blasting them so hard it made him stagger a little. The storm was letting up just enough to make it so they weren't walking blind, but it was still incredibly dangerous to attempt hiking in these conditions.

After walking a short distance out onto the glacier, Jonah stopped and Val followed suit. Her hand had still been on his shoulder, but as she turned toward him, she let it fall away. The space where her hand had been suddenly felt cool and empty, and he wished for it back. But there was no time to waste.

"We need to build a wall to block the wind," he told Val, talking loudly so she could hear him in the storm.

She looked as if she were going to argue for a moment, but instead nodded. He was grateful he didn't need to convince her, since every second they stood there was another second closer to one or both of them getting hypothermia.

She seemed to understand this, too, and they began working in the snow with urgency. He was relieved to see that they could easily work together without talking, because it would've been nearly impossible to do so, even though the storm seemed to be lightening up a little. Luckily, Val knew her stuff, and soon they had a partial cave built out of snow to huddle in. It was rudimentary, not a full snow cave, but if the storm was short-lived, it would be all they'd need. And if it started getting worse, he was confident they would be able to make their shelter something they could overnight in if necessary.

The two of them huddled into the tiny space. Jonah could breathe a bit easier now that they were out of immediate danger, and he could feel Val beside him, her body pressed against his, small but not fragile in the least. As his body calmed and rested after all the exertion, he watched her, absorbing the expression of confident determination on her face. He could see that she still had no doubt they would make it to the summit, and he couldn't help but believe her, despite the difficulties they had faced. She really was extraordinary, indomitable, and Jonah counted himself lucky to be up there with her, even in a snowstorm.

She seemed to feel his eyes on her and turned toward him.

Their faces were only inches apart, and Jonah stared into her eyes in the dim light. His breath caught in his throat as the power of her gaze coursed through him. He leaned closer and reached up to move a strand of hair from her face, wanting to feel her soft cheek against his fingers, wanting to feel her lips against his. But before he could touch her, she lowered her eyes and turned away. His hand hung in midair for a second before he dropped it to his side and leaned away, mortified at his actions.

"We need to get warm and eat something," she said, not looking at him.

Jonah wanted to apologize profusely for making her feel uncomfortable, promise to keep his distance as best he could while huddling together for warmth, but his brain couldn't form the right words, and Val didn't seem interested in discussing it, anyway. She dug into her bag and pulled out her heavy jacket and a space blanket. "If we put on our jackets and each wrap up in our blankets, we should stay plenty warm until this lets up," she said.

Now Jonah felt chagrined for a few more reasons. He almost didn't want to tell her the truth because he knew what her reaction would be. "I didn't bring a blanket," he said, embarrassed.

She turned toward him and her shock was obvious. "You didn't?"

"I only have extra pairs of socks and my jacket," he confessed with a grimace.

He knew what that expression on Val's face meant before she said anything else. It was a cross between fury and panic, and he felt ashamed of himself. She shook her head. "You were going to hike solo and didn't bring extra supplies for emergencies? Jonah…"

He knew how stupid that was, and he waited for her to berate him, but after a few seconds she seemed to think better of it. "Well, nothing we can do about that now," she said, shrugging her shoulders and preparing to wrap her own blanket around both of them as he pulled on his jacket.

He was relieved, but also felt she was being kinder than he deserved and felt guilty that she would need to spend time closer to him than she'd like. If he'd brought his own blanket, they could stay warm without needing to touch, which she clearly preferred.

He hadn't been all that concerned about himself when he'd packed for this trip, and he regretted that behavior and wouldn't have blamed her for being mad at him. But it seemed she wasn't going to say anything more about it, and they both retrieved snacks and water from their packs. Their shoulders and sides touched as they huddled under the single blanket, but Jonah was careful to avoid creating any more discomfort for this woman he held in such high esteem. He had already made enough mistakes for one day.

His mind kept going back to that earlier moment, where everything but her jade eyes had faded away into nothingness. There was a spark there that he couldn't deny, even if only to himself. Just being near her made his heart pound heavily, in a way that had nothing to do with the altitude or physical exertion.

Jonah felt as if he were attuned to every move she made, and their connection was so strong that they seemed like the only two people in the world. But she clearly didn't feel the same, and he'd need to accept that. Really, it was the best for everyone, himself included.

Still, his heart continued to beat fast, and he couldn't stop noticing each of her breaths, every movement she made, as if they were all that mattered. And with so many thoughts like this unspoken, and that near touch that she'd averted, the air hung thick between them despite the gusts of swirling snow.

Val didn't know what to say to Jonah, and it seemed he felt the same way because the silence continued unbroken except for the occasional crunch of a granola bar or crinkle of a wrapper. Staring into his eyes had been electrifying, and that scared her more than the falling boulders and impenetrable snowfall they had experienced not so long ago.

She had feelings for this man and wished she could have allowed that earlier moment to continue unbroken. But she knew she couldn't start dating, and she was more than a little concerned about his decision-making right now. She still couldn't believe he'd brought so little for this hike and feared that his sister's loss was making him do stupid things, like nearly kissing a woman he hardly knew.

She had to tell herself it was his grief and not true feelings that had caused that moment, because otherwise her heart might not be able to bear it. And because she would probably only get hurt if she allowed herself to think he might be falling for her.

She knew she had feelings for him, and if she believed he actually felt the same way, it would make everything else that much harder. They couldn't be together, not in any capacity. And she would need to tell him that, though she dreaded the idea of saying those words and dashing the possibility of a life with him, as foolish as she knew she was being.

He had his grief to face and she had her diagnosis. It wasn't a time to try to start something. They would summit the mountain once the storm calmed, finish this hike, and that would be it for them.

As if in answer to that last thought, Jonah broke the long silence. "We'll need to wait and see if this is just a quick blast. If it is, we might still be able to summit. If it lasts longer than a couple hours, though, we'll need to head straight back down once it blows itself out."

Val felt her throat constrict at that possibility. "We *have* to summit," she said, to him and God and the mountain itself.

The expression on his face told her what she already knew. Sometimes people didn't make it, and that was simply a fact of the hike. She knew that. But for her, there might not be another chance, and she needed to do this before it was too late. She had faced so many obstacles already, and she had always believed she would make it. She wasn't about to stop believing that now because of a little snowfall.

"Val, if this storm doesn't let up, there's a chance we'll be stuck here for days. There's that other storm on its way," he reminded her quietly.

Val had faith, though. God knew how much she needed this.

"God answers prayers," she told him. "Let's just eat and watch the snow and wait to see what happens. When the weather clears up, we can get moving again," she finished, looking at him for confirmation.

Jonah nodded but she could see he was hesitant, that he thought she was too hopeful in the face of all this snow.

"Don't worry," she said, "I understand we can't get to the top if this gets worse. I just believe God is listening."

He still seemed a bit skeptical. "Well, you did pray that the snow wouldn't get any worse out on Disappointment Cleaver. God seemed to miss that one," he said with a little humor.

Val gave Jonah a smile and a shrug. "I guess He

knew better than I did what I needed there," she told him.

He chuckled but didn't answer.

Val just couldn't face the possible loss of this goal she had worked so hard for. No, in her heart of hearts she was sure she would finish this hike, and she couldn't possibly accept that this could be the end. So she simply sent up yet another silent prayer for the snow to stop soon, and then she focused on what she could control: stay warm, eat, drink water.

Jonah didn't press the topic and they sat in silence, munching on their meal of energy bars, beef jerky, chocolate and dried fruit. Val kept watching the snow fall. It was definitely coming down lighter now, and she knew they would be starting their hike again soon, and they would make it to the top.

Intellectually she'd known she might not summit for any one of a million reasons, and before her diagnosis, she would have simply vowed to try again. But now she knew that if she didn't reach the peak today, she might never make it, and she couldn't accept that.

For a few seconds she was bursting to tell Jonah everything, to explain why she broke away from him before and why this was all so important to her and why she would *not* give up, but in the end she just couldn't. She even turned slightly and opened her mouth, but no words came out. Looking at his care-worn face was enough to stop her. He was dealing with so much already, and she didn't want to add her burdens to his. She shifted again, and he glanced at her, but she forced her eyes to stay fixed on her beef jerky, and eventually he turned back to his own snack. Her heart ached as the moment passed, but it was better this way.

She knew she needed to share the truth with someone, though. The only ones she had talked to about it were the doctor, her boss and God. She'd been planning on telling Clayton and Ellie as they made their way back down the mountain together today, before their plans had been dashed by Ellie's altitude sickness. It had seemed like the best idea to tell them after they'd made it to the summit so they wouldn't worry about her before or during the hike, though she felt guilty for keeping them in the dark. It had all happened so fast.

She still couldn't believe it had only been two weeks ago that her doctor had told her she had stage three breast cancer. Even though she'd known what they were testing for, the diagnosis had hit her like a ton of bricks. She'd gone from the healthiest she'd ever been to a cancer patient in a matter of seconds.

Suddenly she was planning days for chemotherapy, consulting with her boss about time off and researching how to make her will, something she'd never considered necessary before, even though her parents had died quite young.

Not that her will took very long. With all her close family gone and no spouse or children, she would just give what she had to her friends and her church. It was a stark reminder that she didn't have many people in her life.

For the past several months, she'd been so focused on work and settling into her home, as well as her hiking goals, that she hadn't had time to feel alone very often. Until she'd received her diagnosis, when it was brought harshly to her attention. The people closest to her were her two friends, whom she cared for deeply, but it wasn't the same as family.

She hadn't realized how much she longed for family.

But she would get through this, she told herself. Chemotherapy often worked. Plenty of people went on to lead full lives after a cancer diagnosis. It would be a hard journey, but with God's help she would manage.

And maybe afterward, if the chemotherapy was successful—*when*, not *if*, she reminded herself—she would give Jonah a call and explain why she'd had to disappear. And perhaps they could go for a hike together. Or a date, if he was still free at that time. The thought of him being unavailable when they could finally be together made her stomach flip unpleasantly, and she pushed that idea away. All she could do was have faith that it would happen for them eventually.

Because the more time she was around him, the clearer it became that he felt like family to her. She connected with him in a way she didn't even with her closest friends, even though she and Jonah had spent so little time together. They just seemed to *fit*. That had been true a year ago and it was true now.

Looking back, he'd been the bar for every unsuccessful date over the past year, every possible person her friends considered setting her up with. And nobody matched him, not even close. Even though she had only known him for a few hours one day a year ago, it had been enough.

She'd been too broken to realize it at the time, but looking back, she could clearly see how deeply those few hours with this man had embedded him into her heart. Right now, however, there was just too much going on to even dream of pursuing a relationship.

She couldn't stop herself from dreaming anyway, though. Or from thinking about how his fingers had nearly grazed her cheek. Even though he hadn't touched her, she could experience it in her imagination and feel the flood of joy as his skin touched hers, their eyes locked. Val knew that little, broken moment would come back to her many times in the months ahead.

She looked over at Jonah, trying to bring herself back to the present. He was looking at his phone, his lips pursed. "Any service?" she asked, already knowing the answer.

He shook his head. "No. I would have been amazed if there was, but I couldn't help checking. It would be great if we could at least send a message that we're safe. I wish we could let your friends know. I'm sure they're worried about you, and sometimes worried people try ill-conceived rescue attempts that do more harm than good."

His concern was evident, and she saw the wisdom in what he was saying. She knew the stories of friends and loved ones injuring themselves or even dying on mountains while searching for others, and she could imagine it happening easily enough. But she had to hope her friends would stay at the camp. "Clay is a smart guy, and he knows exactly how much I've trained for situations like this. I'm sure he trusts that I made it somewhere safe," she said, as much to ease her own fears as his.

Jonah tilted his head. "Clay Williams?"

Val raised her eyebrows in surprise. "Yeah, he's who I came with today, along with our other friend, Elisabeth Mendoza. Ellie. You know Clay?"

Jonah smiled. "Yeah, I do. We've done a couple hikes together. Met once doing segment J of the Pacific Crest Trail a few years back, and he was such a good guy that we ended up planning a few more that summer. Fell out of touch by the next summer, but he was fun to walk with. I can see why you two would be close. Small world."

"Small world," Val said, thinking about what she'd learned. Clay had known Jonah all this time. Even if they hadn't spoken in years, he probably still had Jonah's phone number or email address. If only she'd figured out her feelings a few months ago and had been willing to share them with the people closest to her…

But that was neither here nor there.

Still, it was nice to know that they had a common friend. And she understood what he meant when he said he could see why they were close. She promised herself to tell Clay how good of a friend he was, right about the time she told him about her diagnosis.

Val smiled at Jonah and their eyes locked again. She could feel electricity charge through her. The air between them felt warm despite the snow falling around them. The sky had brightened enough that she could see the color of his eyes, and she found herself getting lost in that deep amber.

He turned away first, and for that she was grate-

ful, because she had been unable to do it herself.
"How do you know Clay?" he eventually asked, taking a last bite of his bar and crumpling up a wrapper.

She silently thanked him for getting the conversation going again, because she had too many things she wanted to say and couldn't say any of them. But talking about her friends was safe.

"Clay actually helped me get my job. I met him out on Mt. Si one day and we started talking, and then I found out he was a writer and he found out I was looking for something in publishing. That was a saving grace in my life, and it's made us so much closer than I think we would be otherwise. I feel truly blessed to know him."

After a second of silence, Val risked another glance at Jonah, and she was confused by his expression. It seemed like disappointment, but why would he—

Oh.

Val could feel her cheeks flush, and even though she knew she couldn't possibly pursue a relationship with him right now, she felt like she had to at least fix the misunderstanding. "He's a really good friend," she continued. "I just hope he gets up the courage to tell Ellie how he feels about her, now that they're stuck at Camp Muir waiting for me. He's been in love with her for such a long time."

The relief on Jonah's face made Val want to do a tiny victory dance. She knew it was going nowhere—it *had* to go nowhere for now—but she couldn't help but tuck that knowledge into a special corner of her heart. Squirrel it away for another time, hopefully, maybe.

"He hasn't ever told her about his feelings?" Jonah asked.

Val shook her head. "The three of us have spent so much time together over the past couple of months, and it's been obvious since the beginning that he's fallen for her, but I think it just never seemed like the right time to him."

"I know how that is," Jonah said so softly Val wasn't sure if she'd actually heard it or just hoped it.

"I think they belong together," she said, talking more to herself than anything else.

"You do?" he asked.

Their eyes met. "I do." Somewhere in the back of her brain, a voice warned her she was on dangerous ground, but it was so hard to hear it when she was looking into his eyes. "It just *feels* right."

Silence surrounded them for a long beat before Val got control of herself. She looked away and scrambled for something to say. "But sometimes it's better not to start something up. You know, if it's not the right time. I know I'm not at a point in my life where I can begin a serious relationship. Not even with someone as wonderful as Keith," she said, attempting a little humor.

It fell flat to her own ears. She wanted to ignore her diagnosis and the future uncertainty and tell Jonah exactly how she felt about him. She didn't even need to look at him to know that he heard the message in her words. His still body beside hers was enough to tell her that he got it all too well, and it broke her heart. She wanted desperately to forget about all the obstacles and say she was falling in love with him.

But she couldn't. He'd been through so much. It was better to keep him at a distance for now, for his sake. It was the kindest thing she could do.

"The snow isn't coming down so hard anymore," she said, trying to get out of dangerous territory. She watched the weather outside their little cave, willing it to go away. "Maybe we can get going again in a few minutes," she finished hopefully.

"Hey," Jonah said, bringing her attention outside herself. She looked at him, and his eyes were calm and confident. "No matter what happens," he told her, their eyes locked, "I will go to the top of this mountain with you."

Val's heart soared and she smiled at him, relieved. He continued, "Even if we get medevaced out of here, we'll try again another day, and you *will* make it to the summit, and I'll be right there with you when you write your name in the book, next to everyone else who made it."

Her heart plummeted again. He didn't know, didn't understand.

"I want to do this with you, Val, even if it's not today, okay?" he told her.

Val's eyes dropped to her lap and she struggled not to cry. She knew he was trying to be reassuring, but each word cut at her heart. She wanted to agree and curl up with him, to ignore her diagnosis and trust that she'd have another chance and that they could do this together, but she held herself apart, letting silence fall between them.

She didn't want to burden him, had used that as her reason to not tell him over and over that day, but her resolve was wavering yet again. He had to know there was something wrong. Maybe it was time to tell him the reason this could be her only chance and why they wouldn't be seeing each other after this.

She couldn't stand the secret anymore. Telling him would add more burden, but not telling him, especially if he had feelings for her, seemed unfair to him. She gathered her courage to tell him the truth, quieting the little voice that kept protesting, telling her to keep it to herself.

Val turned toward him yet again, this time careful not to look into his eyes, trying not to think too much. He shifted, too, and she could feel him watching her, waiting to hear whatever she had to say. Val took a deep breath, preparing herself to shatter her imaginary world where they left the mountain together, hand in hand, ready to try again another day. Or the one where they parted at the bottom with him none the wiser and content to be so.

I have cancer and that's why we can't be together even though I think I'm in love with you.

The words she needed and hated to say were on the tip of her tongue, ready to spill out of her, when a strange sound broke the stillness around them—a scraping, snuffling noise Val couldn't identify. The moment broken, Val and Jonah turned their attention to the empty glacier spread out before them. The snow wasn't falling very fast at all anymore, and Val peered through it, trying to make out what could have made that sound. She wondered if it was possibly one of those hikers they'd met out on The Flats or perhaps someone lost out on the glacier, but that didn't match what she was hearing. Whatever it was, it just didn't sound human.

In the dim dawn light, she finally spotted it amongst the rocks and snow, a dark crouched figure moving slowly, probably fifty feet away, in the direction they had come from, near Disappointment Cleaver. It was clear enough to make out exactly what it was despite the snow falling around and on it, but her brain struggled to process what she was seeing. Whatever she might have expected that noise to be, it certainly wasn't this. Val heard her breath in her throat as she gasped out, "Is that a…"

She knew what she wanted to say, but it just didn't make any sense. She shook her head a little and squinted at it, hoping that seeing the thing that way might make it less incomprehensible.

"It's a mountain lion," Jonah said quietly, sounding just as perplexed as she was.

That's what it was, alright: the big sand-colored cat couldn't be mistaken for anything else. She knew enough about mountain lions—pumas, cougars, whatever you want to call them—from safety warnings about certain hikes. They lived around here, and precautions needed to be taken when hiking through their habitat.

But her mind still couldn't accept that what she was seeing was true, because this was definitely not its habitat. They were far above the tree line, out on a glacier. There was no food here for a mountain lion to survive on. So what was it doing all the way up here? And why was it jerking around like that? Something was very, very wrong.

Chapter Five

Jonah watched the large animal, stunned and trying to wrap his head around what he was seeing. He knew there were mountain lions on Mt. Rainier, of course, but not this high up. *Never* this high up.

This was not good.

"It's injured," Val whispered. "Look at the way it's moving."

Jonah watched and immediately saw what she meant. It thrashed its head around as it shuffled forward. It was moving quickly, but the movements were scattered and unpredictable, not like the normal stalking smoothness he'd expect of a cat. Jonah couldn't identify exactly what the problem was, but it was clear that it was hurt.

"I wonder if it got injured and then lost, or if it sustained an injury as it tried to find its way back home. It must've gotten out of its territory days ago to get this high up," he said softly, still trying to understand what he was looking at. He couldn't tear his eyes from the animal.

Then he felt adrenaline shoot through his body as he realized two things at once: the first was that the animal must be absolutely starving, and the second was that it was definitely heading in their direction.

He also felt something he hadn't experienced since before his sister died: fear for his own life. It was hardly noticeable beneath his fear for Val's safety, which was nearly overwhelming all on its own, but it was there.

He could hear Val's breath speed up and knew she saw that it was coming their way, too. And what it could mean if it reached them.

Animals could be unpredictable and dangerous if they considered a human a threat. An animal out of its territory, confused, hurt and very hungry, was something even more worrisome, and they wanted to stay as far away from it as possible. Most mountain lions wouldn't approach people if they could help it, preferring to keep their distance, but they couldn't afford to assume that was what would happen here.

And it was still coming their way, moving a whole lot faster than Jonah would like, even with its injuries.

"We need to get out of here," he said to Val, forcing himself to stop staring at the animal and move. Val turned her attention to her things and packed as rapidly as possible and he did the same. They both knew leaving their gear could spell death out on the glacier, but there was no time to waste.

"We should leave any open food," she said. "And any meat."

He immediately saw the wisdom in her words. The food was probably what was drawing its attention to them in the first place. For it to be this high up, it had to have been wandering without anything to eat for days. And if the mountain lion did smell their food and they packed it all along with them, it would just follow them.

With how fast it was moving, they might not be able to outrun it out there, at least not safely, what with the wind still gusting, their heavy bags and the fatigue from their time out on the mountain in the thin air without a real meal. He couldn't guarantee that they'd move faster than that animal if it was tracking them, and that was a scary thought. Better to leave the food and hope that would be enough.

He dug into his backpack and tossed all the opened food and his stash of beef jerky into a pile before continuing to shove everything else into his bag. Normally the rule was to never leave trash behind, but there simply wasn't time now, and he wouldn't want any wrappers with a lingering scent in his pack anyway. He silently promised to clean up litter the next chance he got and closed the top of his bag.

Val had added several things to the pile, too, and began the last of her preparations. Jonah hoped the heap of bars and beef jerky would be more enticing to the animal than the people who had left it. He glanced again at the mountain lion, trying to gauge the distance between it and them. It couldn't be more than thirty feet away now. He sped up, getting his crampons on and standing up, tossing his backpack onto his back with one smooth motion.

Another glance. Closer, it was definitely closer. He wanted to watch it and see if he could understand what injuries the animal had sustained, but that wasn't an option. Too many other things to do. He did a last check for his safety gear. Ax at his waist, GPS tracker in his pocket, lead rope at the ready. Jonah thought for a second and pulled the GPS tracker back out and saved the current coordinates—they would be useful when talking to rangers.

By the time he was done, Val was standing beside him, ready. She squeezed his arm and he looked at her, their eyes locking. This time, though, it wasn't a shot of electricity that went through him, but fear. He could see the worry in her eyes, but there was also confidence, though he didn't know if it was confidence in him, in herself or in God. Whoever she trusted, he would do everything in his power to help her stay safe. There was no way he could fail her like he failed Becca.

Before they started off, he looked down the mountain at the cougar again and his blood pumped even faster. Twenty feet, maybe. They needed to move before it got any closer. If it saw their movements as threatening, it could attack, and who knew what it could do, regardless of its injuries.

Hardly any time had passed since they'd first spotted the creature, but it felt like far too long. Jonah glanced once more at Val and she nodded. Time to leave their little shelter. Jonah had hoped their stop would be fairly short, but he had never imagined it ending quite like this, with a mad dash away from a wild animal.

But that was the situation at hand. A quick prayer for Val's safety and it was time to get away from there. He shot another glance at the cougar. He could hear its heavy breathing, see the way its ribs stood out through its fur, which looked patchy and not nearly warm enough for the temperatures up so high. Even though Jonah was still very attuned to the danger of the situation and was aware of the damage it could do if it wanted to, he also felt sorry for the poor thing. He would help it if he could, but for now the only thing he could do was get Val as far away from it as possible.

They hadn't had time to secure the lead rope properly, and Jonah was worried about getting separated before they could stop and fix the problem, so he grabbed Val's hand, holding it tightly in his own. Then they began moving in the opposite direction of the creature, trying to put distance between it and themselves as quickly as they could, sparing occasional looks back to see what it was doing. Jonah's legs burned and the gusting wind chilled his skin, but resting now wasn't an option. They needed to keep going; there was no other option.

Jonah knew that it would be better if they could go back down the mountain, get help for the creature right away and give up on their trip to the summit, but that way was blocked. The mountain lion was coming exactly from that direction and Jonah knew that trying to skirt around it would be risky. Going farther out onto the glacier would risk them getting lost or falling into a crevasse. The only direction they could safely go was up toward High Break and the summit.

Now that he could actually think a little about this rather than going on necessity and instinct, Jonah felt both anxious and relieved by that. He knew how desperately Val wanted to reach the summit, and with everything that had happened so far, he couldn't help but be happy that her dream was still within reach.

He was also aware of the dangers that created. They were low on food, and they now had a cougar in the way of their path back down the mountain, a situation which was unlikely to get better just because they managed to reach the summit.

Jonah didn't know what to do about any of those issues, and right now the important thing was to put one foot in front of the other, to get distance between them and the animal, to get Val someplace safer—so that's what he did. He would figure out step two later.

He glanced back once again at the mountain lion and was relieved to see that its attention was clearly on the wrappers and food instead of on them. When he saw it stop and bury its muzzle into the beef jerky, he whispered a prayer of thanks as some of the tension left his shoulders. He vaguely noticed that he was praying again, but shelved that thought for another time, too. Jonah knew they weren't safe yet, and the animal could change its mind at any minute. He kept moving, still holding tightly to Val's hand.

Jonah could hear Val beside him, her breath as ragged as his. Even though they'd had a break, the fear and the rush to pack had left them both winded and in desperate need of more rest. But this was no time to stop and catch their breath.

He kept glancing back at the animal, constantly expecting it to decide they were more interesting, but it didn't, and soon they were far enough away that Jonah could no longer see it through the snowfall. It seemed like the cougar must have decided their leftovers were a good enough haul and it wouldn't be following them. But it wasn't worth it to stop and find out for sure.

The snow continued to fall around them, but lightly enough that Jonah wasn't too worried about visibility in the gray morning light. They still weren't remotely out of danger yet, though. They were continuing on into thinner and thinner air, with less food than before and no prospect of a break anytime soon. But for this moment, they could relax a little bit and slow their pace enough to catch their breath, though Jonah was not about to stop walking until they'd put a safe distance between them and the animal, unless it was absolutely necessary.

"How are you doing?" he asked Val. "Do you have enough energy to keep going for a while?"

Val chuckled, though her breathing was still gaspy. "Trust me, after what just happened, my heart is pumping plenty hard enough to keep me moving for a while. Though we should take a second to get the lead rope tied," she added.

Jonah realized that he was still holding her hand

and tried to ignore the pang he felt as he let go. They were just going to be friends—he knew that. Securing the rope to their belts, they continued on.

They walked in silence, trudging farther and farther up the mountain. Every step felt slow and inconsequential, but he could see that they were reaching High Break, just a short distance from the peak. Even more importantly, they had risen above the storm. The sky cleared as they left the clouds behind, and early morning greeted them with soft blue skies. As they'd walked, Jonah had glanced back every few minutes, but when almost an hour had passed and there was no sign of anything behind them, it felt safe to stop and rest.

He stopped walking and shook his head, trying to understand what had happened and failing. "A mountain lion," he said, finally breaking the silence. It felt like it was hitting him for the first time now that they truly seemed to be safe. "We saw a mountain lion."

Val slipped off her backpack and sat down, stretching out her legs in front of her and grimacing as she massaged her sore muscles. "I knew this hike was going to be exciting, but I never imagined it would involve running away from dangerous animals," she told him.

He dropped to the ground beside her and laughed, relief and joy coursing through him, wiping away a little of his exhaustion. Nothing mattered except that Val was safe, and here she was, joking and alive and as wonderful as ever. "Me neither. I've seen a lot of things, but never a cougar on the top of Mt. Rainier. That's a new one," he said. "I guess we better watch out for rabid marmots next," he finished, mostly to himself.

Val gave him a look that made it clear just how confusing a statement that had been. "A marmot? You mean like a groundhog thing?"

Jonah smiled at the memories that flooded him, knowing how ridiculous it would all sound, but sure that Val would understand. "My sister used to talk about being careful out here and all the different dangers I might meet on my mountain adventures. You know, slipping on a rock face, falling into a crevasse, being buried in an avalanche, that sort of thing. She wanted to be sure that I was prepared and knew how to get out of any sticky situation so I would come home safely."

He saw the expression on Val's face and knew she was thinking about his lack of preparedness for the whiteout and felt guilty. Becca would've been disappointed in him, too. He silently vowed to never do something stupid like that again before he continued his story.

"At some point through the years, she came up

with this idea that marmots were secretly poisonous and out for blood, and it became this weird inside joke between us. Every time I talked to her before a big hike, she'd warn me to watch out for gangs of angry marmots prowling around looking for victims. She once made up a whole ridiculous story about them creating this elaborate plan of attack to catch their unsuspecting prey. Like raptors in *Jurassic Park*, only—"

"Only big furry squirrels." Val finished the thought for him with a little smile.

He smiled back and shrugged his shoulders. "Twins are strange, what can I say?"

"She sounds funny," Val commented.

Jonah felt a wave of pain wash over him. It was still so hard to believe he'd never hear her on the phone again, warning him that she refused to climb a mountain to rescue him, so he'd better be ready for any danger, including bloodthirsty rodents. "Yeah, she was hilarious," he said softly, feeling his throat constrict.

Val's heart ached for Jonah as she saw his shoulders slump under the weight of grief. She could see how much it hurt him to use the past tense when he was talking about his sister, and she couldn't stay silent and watch as he got sucked into his hurt without trying to help somehow, but she was at a loss for words. What could she say against all that pain?

God, please help me find the right words to help soothe his heart, she prayed.

"People don't ever leave us," she told him, saying the only thing that came to mind.

He didn't look at her, just shook his head a little in exasperation. "I know," he said with a sigh. "Everyone reminds me that she's in Heaven looking down on me. That doesn't stop how hard it is right now, though."

"That's not exactly what I meant," she told him, resting her hand on his arm.

He tilted his head, clearly not sure where she was going.

"Yes, there's that, and I'm sure she's watching over you, keeping an eye out for dangerous squirrels," she said, seeing his mouth twitch a little with humor. "But I'm talking about your memories of her. All of those memories have left an impression on your soul. You carry her around with you. It's like that E. E. Cummings poem."

He stared blankly at her. Val paused, too, and took a sip of water before continuing.

"The poem says,

'i carry your heart with me (i carry it in my heart) i am never without it (anywhere I go you go, my dear...'"

Val stopped talking again, watching him. He didn't say anything. She added, "My parents and grandmother were all so important in my life, and I miss them every day, but I'm grateful, too. Grateful for the time I had with them. Every time I bake cookies for Christmas or say the Serenity Prayer, I think about my grandmother. And whenever I hear 'My Girl,' I feel like my parents are with me again, and that's a wonderful feeling. I miss them, but they're watching over me and I'm okay," she said.

She waited for a long while, wondering what he would say, but he just looked away from her back down the mountain. He seemed lost in thought, and she watched him for some sign of what those thoughts might be. His expression gave nothing away, though, so she forged ahead.

"All I'm saying is God gave her to you for years and years, and so even though she's gone now, you had all that time with her, and that's pretty amazing. Every time you climb a mountain, you'll think about deadly marmots and she'll be right there with you. You can't change what happened, but maybe you can change how you look at it."

She trailed off, wondering if she'd offended him. She knew it was hard to give up grief and could only hope he would be able to accept her thoughts the way they were meant, even if it was more than a little presumptuous to tell someone how to handle their sadness after such a short time. Jonah still said nothing, and the longer the silence went on, the more she wished she'd kept her thoughts to herself.

Eventually, he turned to look at her, his expression still inscrutable. He opened his mouth and she readied herself for whatever backlash he might give. Or perhaps he'd just ignore everything she'd said and pretend it hadn't happened and talk about the next part of the hike. She could only wait and listen.

"You just have E. E. Cummings poems memorized, huh?" he asked.

She laughed in surprise at that unexpected response, then shrugged. "I was an English nerd in high school and I work in a publishing house. It just happens sometimes. I can also throw out some pretty impressive Shakespeare monologues if necessary," she said.

"I'm sure that comes in handy at parties," he said with a chuckle.

"Exactly," she responded, and a friendly silence fell between them.

Val held out her hand, and Jonah took it, her gloved hand nestled in his, their eyes meeting. "It'll always hurt. I know that from experience. But from what I know about her, I'm sure your sister would want you to keep smiling and to have a happy life.

And like all those other people keep reminding you, I truly believe you'll see her again."

The moment lingered between them as they stared at one another. She didn't let herself think about what that might mean, just allowed herself to be present and enjoy it.

"Thanks," he finally said. "And you're right. It will just take me time to get to a place where I'm okay."

"Yeah, it will," she agreed. She bit back more words, words about wanting to be there for him as he fought through the difficult times. She wanted desperately to help and be an anchor when he struggled.

But she couldn't say those kinds of things. She didn't know if she would be around for anyone for all that long. Even just the next few weeks, she wouldn't be able to help anyone, probably not even herself. Those harsh truths meant she had nothing to offer him.

So she kept quiet and instead focused on the feel of their hands intertwined. They were far enough away from the mountain lion to be out of danger, and neither seemed in a rush to break away and continue the hike. Val let her soul settle into that place where they were connected. If she couldn't have more than this moment, she would need to let this, here, be enough. She would carry these memories of Jonah in her heart.

It was time to finish that final small hike up to the peak, and even though Val was ecstatic to do so, it was hard to break their connection. Reluctantly, she let go of Jonah's hand, and she tried to compose herself before they began the last push toward the summit. She wished they could have stayed that way for much longer, but they couldn't afford to waste more time, and Columbia Crest—the top of Mt. Rainier—was so close it made her feel jittery with anticipation. So she focused on preparing to accomplish her goal and not on how bare her hand felt when it wasn't enfolded in his. "Will you be ready to leave in a few minutes?" she asked him, grabbing the last of her granola bars.

Jonah gave her a pained look, as if he didn't want to say what he had to say. "Val, we need to stay put so the helicopter can come get us," he said, taking out his GPS tracker.

The words took Val by complete surprise, and she struggled to comprehend them. "What do you mean?" she asked, hoping she wasn't understanding him correctly. Praying he wasn't saying they should stop when they were so close to accomplishing their goal.

The expression on his face made it clear he regretted his words. "We can't keep going, Val. We've got to use the GPS to send our coordinates. The helicop-

ter can come get us and take us off the mountain. It's
the only safe way. Don't forget, we're low on food.
If that storm coming tomorrow decides to hit early
or if anything else goes wrong, the helicopter might
not be able to help us."

Val shook her head. They had to finish their hike;
there was no other option in her mind. They had
come so far, and they were almost there. "We're so
close. If we just hurry…" She trailed off as she saw
the truth in his eyes. "We *need* to summit," she told
him, out of arguments.

When Jonah spoke, his voice was soft. "Val, I've
tried to think of some other way, but there isn't one.
We also have to think about the mountain lion. We
need to make sure no other hikers cross its path, and
get it medical attention as soon as possible. Now that
we're safe, those two things are more important than
making it to the summit. We have to tell the rangers
so they can get up here and do something."

She'd been so focused on getting away from the
animal that it had never occurred to her, but of course
they had to help it if they could. "You don't think
they'll *kill* it, do you?" she asked, her forehead wrin-
kling with worry at the idea of that poor animal being
put down.

"I think they will do everything they can to help
it get healthy and back home if it's at all possible,"

he reassured her. "And the sooner they find it, the more likely that will be."

Val bowed her head. She knew he was right, and she didn't want to be the reason that creature wasn't helped in time. It was hard to say goodbye to the dream of reaching the top of Mt. Rainier, especially when she was so very close, but she knew that she couldn't fight him anymore, that he was right.

There had always been the possibility something would stop her from getting to the summit, and she'd been well aware of it long before her friends had decided not to attempt it that morning, but that had never stopped her from being so sure she would make it somehow.

Jonah pushed a few buttons on his GPS tracker, sending out the SOS message and their coordinates. Val watched, defeated. Then he put the gadget in his pocket and took her hand again, giving it a little squeeze to get her attention. "You'll have another chance, Val," he told her reassuringly. "I promise we'll come back."

At those words the tears came hot and fast, and suddenly she was in his arms, sobbing. She didn't know which of them reached out first, and it didn't matter. What mattered was his strength surrounding her, protecting her, just like it had during the earthquake, as she fell to pieces.

She cried because they wouldn't be coming back, and because she'd be apart from him so soon, and because she had cancer, and because his sister died, and because of all the difficulties on their hike that forced them to give up after getting so far. She let it all wash over her and come out in the tears she'd never cried at the doctor's office or when making her will or any of the other times when she should have cried and didn't.

She was finally letting herself cry because it was safe and comforting in his arms. She felt sure he would hold her as long as she needed, but soon she had passed through the storm, risen above it just as they had the storm on the mountain. Val took a deep breath, trying to calm her breathing, leaning her cheek against his chest. His voice rumbled through her as he said the old, comforting words. "'God, grant me the serenity to accept the things I cannot change,'" he said, "'the courage to change the things I can—'"

"'And the wisdom to know the difference,'" she finished with a little sigh. He was right. The words were right.

A feeling of calm washed over her, and she felt better than she had since the doctor's office. She hadn't even realized the weight she'd been carrying until the load felt lighter, and she breathed easier than she had in weeks.

She wasn't going to make it to the top of Mt. Rainier that day, and she couldn't change that. But she could accept it, and she could decide how she chose to look at it.

"I'm so grateful I got this far," she told both him and herself, not moving from his embrace, her head still on his chest. "And that I got to experience it with you."

The arms around her tightened, and they sat there pressed together for a long minute. She would remember this moment fondly when they were apart, she told herself, thanking God for it as she savored the closeness to someone she held so dear.

"There's still plenty of time left this season for another attempt," Jonah said, looking down at her, his eyes filled with sincerity. "How about we try again in a couple weeks?"

Val knew he was trying to help, but tears began threatening to fall once more, so she just shook her head. He seemed to understand enough not to push the subject.

In a couple weeks she might be too worn down to climb stairs at a decent pace, let alone hike a mountain, if chemotherapy was as rough as she'd heard it could be. But she would trust in God and maybe someday, if He willed it, she'd try again.

Then she took a breath and moved out of the embrace, wiping the tears from her eyes as she settled in to wait. "How long do you think it'll take for the helicopter to get here, and what do you think we should do while we wait?"

There were plenty of things he'd like for them to do, like talk about why she wasn't interested in trying the hike again another day and what exactly was going on inside her head, but her eyes still threatened tears, and he wasn't about to make this moment more difficult for her than it needed to be.

"There's no telling how long it'll take. It depends on the storm and other stranded hikers and plenty of other factors," he told her. She nodded, and he continued, "As far as what to do while we wait, you can quote more poetry if you like."

His attempt to lighten the mood was rewarded with a chuckle and a relieved smile. They settled in the snow beside each other, waiting for the helicopter to come find them based on the sent coordinates.

Jonah watched Val out of the corner of his eye, trying to understand her. Anybody who climbed Mt. Rainier knew failure was a possibility no matter how prepared you were. Things happened. Not usually rogue mountain lions, but hikers were forced to give up for plenty of other reasons. From everything he'd seen of her character during this hike, he would expect her to be upset, sure, but then to try again as soon as possible.

There was clearly something else going on, something much bigger than this one summit attempt, but she didn't seem ready to talk about it and he didn't want to push. And he knew not to tell her how much it meant to him that she was willing to cry in his arms and wished he could be there for her like that long into the future. That wasn't what she wanted to hear—she had made that clear enough already.

Jonah waited, hoping Val might decide to talk, to tell him what burden she was dealing with, but she stayed silent. After a while, when it seemed clear she wasn't going to share her secrets, he talked about the only other thing on his mind.

"Becca always thought this mountain thing of mine was crazy. Whenever I talked to her about which mountain I'd be summiting, she would wish me luck and then tell me she planned to stay on flat ground where she belonged," he said.

Val laughed, and Jonah smiled at the sound as well as his memories. "She did always love the pictures, though. I'd send her a couple after every trip. A cool view, some rocks that looked like a face, and always one from the highest point I managed. Sometimes that would be the top and sometimes it wouldn't. Either way, she'd be mad at me if I forgot to document it for her."

He was going to miss that.

"I remember that from Mt. Si," Val commented.

Jonah sighed as memories flooded him. He looked out at the view around him, the sky a vivid blue, the sunshine glinting off the snow and the wet rocks jutting from the mountainside. In the distance he could see other mountains, including Mt. St. Helens. It was a beautiful view. He glanced at Val and was sure she had the same idea he did. "Would you take a picture with me? I know Becca won't see it, but…"

Val smiled. "Yes, of course. That sounds like a tradition worth keeping up."

Jonah pulled out his phone and they scooted closer together. In the first picture, Jonah's face looked more like a grimace than a grin, as he thought about how his sister wasn't ever going to see it. Val looked at the picture and then at him. "Let's try that again," she said, wrapping an arm around him and waiting.

He put his arm across her shoulders and held the phone up once more, and this time he found himself genuinely smiling, for long enough to take a picture at least. He knew if Becca could have seen that photo, she would have had so much to say, so many questions that would have required answers about how he'd managed to find that pretty girl again. And she would've been so excited, regardless of anything he said about Val just being a friend. Because she would've seen right through that just like she had with the picture a year before.

He put down the arm holding his phone but didn't remove the other from where it rested on Val's shoulder. She didn't take hers off him, either. Jonah looked into her eyes. "Thank you," he said softly, losing himself in those green eyes of hers. His heart pounded.

He wanted so badly to tell her just what he thought when he looked into her eyes. Like everything would turn out okay and God was good. Like he'd found a place to call home.

But, just as before, she looked away after a couple of seconds, turning her eyes back to the view. Her arm dropped away from his waist, and she shifted her body so their hips were no longer touching. Jonah reluctantly took his arm from around her shoulders and returned it to his side.

It felt strange just hanging there like that. Wrong. There was something more going on than Val being uncomfortable with what she'd seen written on his face when they looked at each other. In fact, he was pretty sure he'd seen the same thoughts written on hers, too.

He needed to find out what was going on, because he simply couldn't ignore what was between them without some sort of discussion, without an explanation. Before he could figure out what to say, though, she said, "So your sister must've seen dozens of pictures from the top of Mt. Si then?"

He nodded, vowing silently to not let her change the subject permanently. Answer her question, then start asking a few of his own. "So many pictures. But I tried to make each one unique for her so it didn't get too boring."

"Like taking one with a random girl at the top of the haystack?" she asked.

"That one did stand out, yeah," he said.

He remembered Becca's reaction to it as if it were yesterday. She had been incredibly excited, and then so disappointed he hadn't gotten the girl's number. If she knew he'd found Val again, there would be no question in his sister's mind that it was fate and a date was required.

He hoped that date would happen soon. That would be a part of the discussion if he had anything to say about it. As the start of his segue, Jonah said, "I think Becca would really like you."

"She would probably be annoyed at us for not getting a picture of that mountain lion before we ran for our lives, though, don't you think?"

Jonah laughed, a real loud genuine surprised laugh, for the first time in a long while, as he imagined his sister's reaction. It felt good to laugh. "Oh, I would never hear the end of that one. 'You let a little thing like dismemberment stop you from taking a picture of a cougar!'"

Val laughed at that, and Jonah couldn't stop grinning. "I'm sure it'd become a running joke. Every time I left for a trip, she would remind me that if I find myself in a perilous situation with a dangerous animal, I need to take a picture before running away."

"Sounds reasonable enough," Val said with a grin of her own.

Jonah almost asked Val to help him remember that on their future trips but stopped himself and sighed, looking out at Mt. St. Helens as his mind whirred. Based on her reaction to the thought of trying to summit another time, it probably wouldn't go over well if he mentioned more hikes together. It was time to find out why that thought was so upsetting to her, because he knew deep in his heart that he wanted her beside him on future trips, and not just as a friend. And the more time they spent together, the more certain he felt. He would love nothing more than to be by her side every time she stepped foot on a mountain. And on the days where she was staying on flat ground, too.

For the rest of his life.

Something about being with her just felt right. When they'd put their arms around each other for the picture, it was as if they belonged like that. If she didn't feel the same, he'd accept that, but he needed to hear her say so before he could let go of that dream.

Jonah turned to Val, taking a deep breath and trying to feel prepared for anything that might come out of the conversation they were about to have.

Looking at her, however, he felt incredibly unprepared for what he saw.

Val's lips were trembling. At first he thought she might be starting to cry again, but then his heart constricted with fear. The rest of her was shaking, too, and her eyes looked sleepy in a way that sent danger signals shooting through his body. They hadn't put their big jackets back on after leaving the mountain lion behind, and despite the sunshine, it was bitter cold. She was probably as wet from the snow as he was, and the lack of movement meant less body heat. He had been so full of adrenaline at first and so focused on emotions afterward that he hadn't noticed the cold, and he imagined the same was true for her.

Those were the kinds of mistakes that led to dangerous situations, like frostbite. Or hypothermia.

Chapter Six

Jonah didn't want to believe what he was seeing, but he couldn't lie to himself. Val was going through the beginning stages of hypothermia.

He was paralyzed with fear for only a second or two before he moved into action, practically diving at her backpack and grabbing at the clasps keeping it shut, trying to keep calm as the panic started to build inside him. He had gotten her away from falling rocks, a snowstorm and a mountain lion, only to get her stranded at the top of the mountain, waiting for a helicopter that might take who knew how long—and then not noticed she was getting hypothermia. It was his job as the more skilled hiker and the lead to keep them safe and he'd failed and it might cost Val her life.

Jonah cut off that line of thinking and stopped berating himself. It would help neither of them if he let those thoughts take hold, if he got so caught up in worry and regret that he couldn't do what needed to be done. His mind needed to be clear and calm so he could work quickly. And he needed to keep her calm, too.

"We need to get you into dry things," he told her, using as soothing a voice as he could manage while he rummaged through her bag, pulling out anything that resembled clothes. Luckily, she had packed well, and he found everything she needed, including a few hand warmer packs. He could've kissed her for being so prepared.

"Don't worry, Val, you did a great job packing and you're going to be warm in just a minute. And the helicopter will be here soon and you'll be safe," he reassured them both, turning back to her with the pile of items in his arms, a smile of relief on his face.

What he saw when he turned to her made the smile drop from his face and his panic try to rise up again before he clamped it down. She had stopped shaking, he could see that immediately, and her eyes were half-closed. His heart dropped into his stomach. If she was no longer shivering, her body was shutting down. She was definitely hypothermic, and every second was crucial. And even if he did everything right from this point on and the helicopter showed up in a couple minutes, it still might not be enough.

"Don't take her, too," Jonah mumbled aloud, moving close to Val with the supplies he had gathered. He didn't know if he was praying, begging or warning, and really, it didn't matter.

Jonah took a calming breath as he closed the distance between them. She needed him right now, and he couldn't do what needed to be done if he was so worried he wasn't thinking straight. He started helping her into her dry things as rapidly as possible, rubbing her feet before replacing each wet sock with multiple layers of dry ones. "This will help, Val," he said to her as he worked. "This will get you warm, I promise."

"It will be okay, Jonah," Val told him, her words slurring slightly. "I don't even feel very cold." She gave him a little sleepy smile that he didn't like one bit.

Jonah knew that it was a bad sign if she didn't feel cold anymore, and her not recognizing that fact was even worse. She had trained enough to recognize signs of hypothermia, he was sure, and if she didn't see what was happening, her mental abilities were being affected. As he continued his ministrations, his rapid-fire mental checklist ran through the stages of hypothermia. First uncontrolled shivering, then feeling warm and confused and tired. If it went like that for too long, loss of consciousness and death could follow.

He strained to hear any sounds of whirring blades, scanned for anything at all that might be a helicopter on the horizon. It should be there any minute, he knew, but if it was grounded for any reason or busy helping others, it could still take too long to be of any help in this situation. He had to do all he could while they waited. He willed it to get there faster, get there *now*. They were trapped at the top of Mt. Rainier, and he could only hope he could do enough until more help arrived.

Jonah started speaking to Val softly, like he would if he were reassuring an injured kid on one of the camping trips he did through the church. Val wasn't scared like a hurt child, but it was mostly for him, not her. It was the only way he could manage to keep the worry down and stay calm for her. "I'm right here, Val. I'm right here with you. We'll get through this together," he told her, repeating the same phrases over and over. He worked on her fingers and hands and arms, trying to create warmth before he added the extra layers.

He watched her carefully for even the slightest changes, and when her eyes began to close, his throat constricted. He needed her awake, needed to know that she was there with him as he helped her into layer after layer. "Hey, Val, talk to me. Tell me something," he said, desperately trying to think of something that would get her talking. "It's been quite the adventure today, huh?"

"I don't want to date Keith," she told him in a sleepy voice.

Jonah wanted to laugh and cry at the same time at that. He wasn't sure that counted as answering his question, but at least the words were coherent. "You don't have to date Keith," he told her soothingly. "To tell the truth, I wouldn't date him, either. He seemed like a bit of a jerk, if you ask me," he said, adding the final outer layers of gloves and shoes to keep the snow off her fresh layers, using every spare bit of clothing she had with her, including one of his own extra pairs of socks. Her shoes would probably feel tight, but cramped toes seemed low on the list of priorities. "Are you feeling any warmer?"

"Everything's going to be fine, Jonah," she said, patting Jonah gently on the shoulder as he continued to make his way through the pile. "Whatever happens, God will be there with me. He'll help me through it, don't you worry."

Jonah didn't think she was talking about Keith anymore, and maybe not about hypothermia, either, but he wasn't going to ask her to explain anything in this state. In all likelihood, she hardly knew what she was talking about any more than he did. But keeping her talking and comfortable was paramount, so he just answered as best he could.

"Of course He'll help you through it," Jonah reassured her, pulling a beanie over her hair and down until her ears were covered. "Keep talking, Val. Tell me whatever you like."

Jonah focused his attention on getting her warm. The fact that she was talking at all, even if it was a little confused, was better than if she fell asleep.

"I'm not scared," she continued. "I just don't want to hurt anyone. I *definitely* don't want to hurt you, Jonah."

"I appreciate that," he responded, his attention more on her voice than her words as he checked the pile of supplies he'd gathered from her pack. He was on the last few things now. He had to hope there would be no lasting damage. That he hadn't waited too long.

He helped her push her arms into her jacket, tucking the activated hand warmers in for added heat, and then he added his own jacket on top.

Please please, God, help her come back.

He didn't realize he was praying until he was repeating the prayer over and over, hoping God would help him. A little bit of calm worked its way through him as he gave some of the control up to a higher power.

Jonah covered them both with a space blanket, the silver sheet crackling as he settled it over them. Now they would just need to wait and keep talking until she felt better or until the helicopter showed up. And all that time, he would silently pray for God's help and hope that it would all be enough.

He huddled up close to Val, wishing he could do

more for her, wishing he had moved faster, been more aware and noticed sooner. None of that helped, and he knew it, but it was hard not to blame himself. He'd been so focused on his own problems, and so had Val, that they'd forgotten basic mountaineering rules. And now Val might pay because of it.

He studied Val, searching for spots where the cold might still seep in. She was bundled up with everything he could possibly put on her. His heart still beat fast, looking for any tiny thing he could do that might tip the scales in her favor. "I'm going to wrap my arms around you, okay, Val?" he asked in a soft voice.

"A hug sounds wonderful," she told Jonah, leaning toward him.

He pulled her close, rubbing her arms through the layers of fabric and trying to get any bit of warmth he could find in himself over to her.

"'God, grant me the serenity to accept the things I cannot change,'" he said, reciting the familiar words.

He hardly noticed he was talking aloud until she started saying the words with him. "'The courage to change the things I can,'" she whispered, "'and the wisdom to know the difference.'"

Jonah thought about young Val, standing in her grandmother's kitchen, reading those words for the thousandth time. "Tell me about your grandmother," he said to her.

So Val talked, her words washing over him. She told him about her weekly sleepovers at YaYa's house, about all the cookies they would make every Christmas, about their summer trips to the ocean. Then she talked about her parents and how close she had been to them. About how they would sing "My Girl" to her every night when she was little. As she talked, he listened and felt all the love and strength in those words, all the while keeping his arms tight around her.

After what seemed like a very long time, though it couldn't have been more than a quarter of an hour, Jonah noticed that her words weren't slurred or sleepy, and that everything she said was making sense. Her voice was still soft, but clear and strong. When she stopped, he waited to see what she might say next. "Thank you," she told him after a short silence. "I hadn't noticed— But you—" She couldn't seem to find the endings to those sentences, but he understood what she meant.

"I didn't do anything you wouldn't have done," he said, his arms still wrapped around her, his breath coming easier as he truly began to believe that she would be alright.

There was a little crackle of the space blanket as she shifted slightly in his embrace, though not breaking away from it, and nodded, silently acknowledging the truth of the statement. "That doesn't mean

I shouldn't thank you for helping me. If you hadn't noticed the early signs of hypothermia…" she began.

He knew how that sentence ended, and he didn't want to hear those words. The thought had loomed large in his mind for too long, been pushed away too many times, for him to hear them said aloud. "You're going to be okay," he said, as much to reassure himself as to reassure her. "You're coherent and it seems like your body temperature is mostly normal," he added, removing a glove and touching her cheek. It was warm, definitely warmer than his chilly fingers. "Do you have frostbite anywhere?" he asked, still watching her carefully.

She pulled off her gloves and tested each fingertip, then removed the many layers of socks and checked her toes, carefully searching for numbness and skin that was too pale or blue.

"A few pins and needles, but I think I'm okay," she said as she slid her foot back into her boot with a couple of layers discarded for comfort, and he felt the tightness in his heart ease a little more. Then she was peering at him. "How are you? You must have been freezing, too," she told him. "And you gave me your socks," she added, holding up the pair of gray socks that were much too large for her.

He considered his own body with some surprise. It was the first time he'd thought of himself since he'd first noticed her shivering, however long ago that had been. He tested his own fingers and toes and was relieved to find some feeling in all of them. All the work to keep her warm had done the same for him, too, and the space blanket was doing a good job keeping their body heat in.

Val seemed relieved, though she handed his socks back insistently, and Jonah put them on his own feet. "You know you can't help someone with hypothermia if you have it yourself, and you don't have a ton of extra clothes to spare," she commented as he did so.

Jonah knew that and felt like he deserved a lot more haranguing than Val seemed about to give him. He had always followed protocol before, taking care of himself first as a matter of safety. But it had been impossible to think of himself when he saw that she was in trouble. She was much too important to him in a way he couldn't explain, not even to himself.

Val shrugged out of his jacket and began speaking in a voice that wasn't angry, but also brooked no argument. "Here's your jacket back. And you should definitely use the hand warmers now that I'm feeling fine."

He took the jacket but hesitated to take her extra heat sources. "You need to stay warm," he told her.

"So do you," she replied, pushing them toward him. "I'm warm enough, and with dry clothes and my jacket, I'll stay that way. It's not going to help me if you start going hypothermic, you know."

He recognized the truth in her words and did as he was told. "We should walk around a bit to get blood flowing, if you're up for it," he said as she stretched out each leg gingerly. She had been bundled into a ball for a while, and he could see that the movement was painful. He hoped she'd be able to walk.

Val agreed, and after they repacked all their excess supplies, she stood. She was a little shaky at first, and honestly so was he—they'd been sitting for a long stretch and their legs had been pushed so much that a bit of cramping was to be expected—but after a short time grimacing and stretching, they were strolling in a small circle around their things.

"This whole day is going to be quite the story to tell," she told him, taking a few shuffling steps as her feet woke back up with the renewed blood flow.

"My most interesting experience on a mountain, hands down," he agreed, talking about way more than just the mountain lion and the hypothermia scare. So much had happened in these few hours, he felt almost like a different person from the one who woke up at Camp Muir and headed out in the dark.

And he had her to thank. He had prayed again, he felt lighter than he had for a long while—and it was all because of Val. Then he thought about what she'd said when she was hypothermic. "You told me quite a bit about your parents. I'm sorry you went through such a difficult experience when you were so young."

She gave a little nod. "It wasn't easy, but I have so much to be thankful for." After a few seconds, she quietly started to hum the gospel, "So much to thank Him for."

Jonah smiled as he recognized the familiar tune, and soon they were both singing, their voices getting louder with each stanza. Jonah's heart felt full, and he let the lyrics wash over him.

And then Val stopped abruptly and grabbed his arm. Jonah stopped, too, and listened. It was the distinctive sound of a helicopter. They looked at each other and then started to search the skies, at first seeing nothing but bright blue above, clouds below and other mountains in the distance. The aircraft got louder every second, and soon it appeared from the other side of the mountain, close and huge and incredibly loud after so much silence.

Jonah was excited to see it but also felt a pang of disappointment. He needed more time with Val. He didn't want this to be over. They looked at each other, and her eyes told him she felt the same way.

She was such a fascinating woman, and her eyes captured his attention in a way no other woman's ever had. Everything about her did.

Without thinking, he leaned closer and pressed his lips to hers. And she leaned forward, wrapping her arms around him, kissing him back. Jonah felt exhilaration beyond anything he'd ever felt, a feeling more uplifting than anything else he had ever found on a mountain.

The moment he kissed her, he wanted to kiss her again and again, to hug her close, to tell her just how dear she was to him. Tell her that he wanted to be with her for the rest of his life if she'd let him.

But then she broke away and turned from him. "I'm sorry," she said. "We shouldn't have done that, Jonah. We *can't* do that."

Jonah closed his eyes as he regained control. "No, I'm sorry," he told her. "I don't know what I was thinking."

Val shrugged. "It's fine," she said, though it really wasn't, that much was obvious. She wouldn't look at him, and her eyes seemed to shine as if she was on the edge of tears again.

Jonah didn't know what to say. He had just experienced a moment of pure joy, and the fear that he'd never be able to experience it again weighed him down.

He had kissed her. Her mind still couldn't wrap itself around what had happened. It was a brief kiss, their lips touching for only a couple of seconds, but the way her heart had reacted, it felt like something much bigger. Too big, in fact. It scared her how right it felt and how happy it had made her. That reaction had sent alarm bells through her, and she'd listened to them and moved away, for Jonah's sake.

The helicopter was big and loud above them, and she turned her attention to it, watching as it landed a few hundred yards away on a small flat expanse of the glacier.

"We should go meet them," Val told him, wanting to keep their attention on anything but the kiss.

He nodded without saying anything and they gathered their things. Soon, they were moving toward the helicopter, and they could see two men climbing out of it and preparing to meet them.

Jonah still hadn't said a word. There was so much tension that Val had to say something to break the silence. But any topic involving herself was dangerous territory for her right now, so instead she racked her brain for something safe. "It'll be good to see my friends again, and make sure Ellie is okay," she said, hoping her voice sounded more lighthearted than she truly was. "I bet they'll be together by the time we get off this mountain. Once they've actually told each other how they feel, they won't have anything stopping them," she said.

"So what's stopping *you*?" Jonah asked with a

hint of exasperation, his voice begging her to share her secrets. He stopped walking and looked at her, and she couldn't help but look back at him, her heart thudding in her ears.

Val's heart stuttered even as her feet continued moving. She knew very well why, though it was sometimes hard for her to remember that. This wasn't the time in her life to fall for anyone, Jonah even more so. He had enough weighing him down, enough difficulty to work through, and she refused to add her health to that list.

As much as her soul fought against the idea, she knew it was best for him if they didn't speak again once they got off the mountain. It was better if they went their separate ways, at least until after she was healthy again. If she managed to get to that point, of course.

But she held on to the hope that someday, perhaps, they would be able to be together. Because as much as she didn't want to fall for anyone, especially him, she had. There was no way to hide that fact from herself. Her heart jumped when they were near each other, and when he spoke, all she wanted was to hear more. Her soul seemed to know him in a way that she couldn't explain, and if she was healthy, she would tell him all these things before they left this mountain.

But she wasn't healthy, and she was going to start

feeling that fact very soon, and she refused to put him through that.

Everything would turn out as it should, even if it might not be exactly how she wanted it to be right this second. She trusted God and would put her faith in Him. She would make the best of what they'd had here on this mountain, thank God for it and hope that perhaps someday they would get another chance.

And she needed to share all this with Jonah, before they reached the helicopter and their time together on the mountain was over. She could hardly breathe as she gathered her courage, afraid of what she would see in his face when she said the truth out loud.

"Hey," Jonah said softly to get her attention. She looked at him and his eyes told her so much. He said, "I don't know what burdens you're dealing with, Val, but I know they're weighing you down, and I'm pretty sure you're carrying them alone. You don't have to do that. You can talk to me about them. I'm not going anywhere."

She opened her mouth to tell him everything—the cancer treatments, how alone she had felt, that when they touched it felt like she'd found the person she was meant to be with, just when she knew she couldn't start a relationship without asking too much of him.

That she loved him, as crazy as that might sound.

But the words wouldn't come. It was too much,

too many things, and it all caught in her throat. How could she say everything she was thinking? He might think he could help carry her load, but he had his own burdens, and if she told him, she would only add to that. She knew it. But it didn't stop her from wanting to share her feelings with the person who made her feel so safe.

After a moment of her tortured silence, he seemed to understand and grabbed her hand, squeezing it tight. "It's okay," he said.

They continued walking hand in hand as she let her mind and heart calm down. She focused on the warmth of him, on the present moment, because right then nothing else mattered all that much. This was what truly mattered, what she would remember forever.

She wouldn't tell him everything, not that she loved him, certainly—that would just make things more difficult—but she did need to tell him the truth. She could finally accept that she would need to be honest, and then she would need to be strong no matter his reaction. She prayed to God for that strength because she knew she couldn't do this on her own.

"I have cancer," she said, pulling her hand out of his grasp and hugging her arms around herself to give her the courage to keep going. She didn't look at him or stop walking, though she heard his steps falter. She kept her eyes on her feet and forced herself to continue talking, because she had more to say and wasn't sure she'd be able to if she didn't keep going right then. "I don't really want to talk about it. I haven't told anybody about it, not even Clay and Ellie yet. I was going to tell them on the hike back today, actually…" Val realized she was starting to ramble and tried to get herself back on topic. "Anyway, it seemed like you should know. That's why I'm upset about not getting to the summit and why we're not…" She couldn't seem to find the right words. "Well, why I'm not willing to start something new right now," she finished.

They walked in silence for a couple of seconds, her words hanging in the air between them. She wanted to look at him and see his reaction, but she kept herself facing forward, her eyes on the snow at her feet. If there was pity in his expression, or disappointment, or so many other emotions, she didn't think she'd be able to take it. She didn't actually have any idea what she wanted to see there. It seemed better not to know.

And then she heard a heavy thump and cry of surprise, and Jonah's form disappeared from her peripheral vision as if he'd been sucked into the ground.

Chapter Seven

V̲al whipped around in search of Jonah and found that his being sucked into the ground wasn't far from the truth. Jonah was near her feet, his body sunk in the glacier. He was grasping desperately at the snow, everything below his chest disappearing into a crevasse that had opened under his feet. His face showed shock and strain as he tried to keep himself from falling in even farther.

"Jonah!" she shouted, fear coursing through her. Then her training kicked in as she absorbed the situation. She threw herself to the ground, thrusting her ice ax into the snow in front of her in self-arrest position, testing it to be sure it was solid and would hold their weight. Both of their lives could depend on that ax, and she was relieved to see she'd sunk it well on the first try.

Crevasses could be deep and dangerous, and there was no way to know whether it went down five feet or twenty. If Jonah fell in, the rope tying them together would drag her in, too, unless she did her job and instead kept her hiking partner as well as herself safe. If the rope was secured well enough, she would be able to haul him out. Both of their lives could depend on some rope and that little ax.

Val felt fear catch in her throat, and she began to run through all the worst-case scenarios. Even if the ax was wedged tightly and could hold their weight, if the lead rope wasn't secure or was too long, they could be separated if Jonah fell, and his life could be in danger. Ice and snow above could crumble, leaving him buried under it and cutting off his air supply.

She took a deep breath and slowed the litany of worries. *God, please get us safely through this*, she prayed, and then she focused her mind on the things she could control.

Her end of the rope was knotted securely at her waist, she knew, but she checked it just to be sure. It held tight. And now her ax was properly secured in the ice, and it appeared to be positioned correctly for the rescue procedures running through her mind. Val had prepared for situations like this over and over again in her safety training courses, and she knew what to do. She could feel anxiety pressing against her mind, wanting her attention, but she pushed down all the fear and worry—if she didn't act quickly, the situation could get much worse, and Jonah could be hurt. Or killed. It was time to gain information and be decisive, not sit there and fret.

"Is your lead rope knotted securely, do you think?" she asked him, praying he'd tied it well and they could use it to help him get out.

Jonah gave her a strained "Yeah," and she had to trust that he knew what he was talking about. There wasn't time to check or to reconsider, because it was obvious he was doing everything he could to keep from falling farther into the empty space below his feet. He clearly couldn't reach his ax or help her at all. It was up to her to get him out of there before he lost his grip and fell, and she had no idea how much time she had.

So Val didn't waste any of it. She tested her ax once more, then began looping the rope around it to create a pulley that she could use to haul Jonah up and out of the crevasse. Her already-tired muscles and lungs burned from lack of oxygen as she went through the steps of a rescue in this high altitude, anchoring herself with ice screws, carabiners and rope. If she didn't do this right, it could end disastrously. She would do it right.

She wanted to look to see if the rescue crew from

the helicopter were on their way to help, but she knew better than to take her eyes off what she was doing, and she couldn't wait and hope they'd seen what had happened. It was up to her and she could do this.

Once everything was ready, she began to pull the rope, watching as it slid over the ax handle, studying it for any signs of weakness or failure. The ax didn't move, and the rope became taut as she began to take Jonah's weight. He was much heavier than she was, but with the pulley she could pull him up all on her own if she had to, even if he lost his grip.

She continued to pull the rope and watched as Jonah, no longer completely dependent on his arm strength to keep him from falling, released his grip on the ground with his right hand. He reached down to his waist and grabbed his own ax. Within seconds he was holding it aloft, and then he slammed it down into the ice in front of him, digging it in as best he could before using it to help pull his weight out of the crevasse.

Val wanted to keep watching him to ensure that he was getting out, but she needed to focus her eyes on the pulley she'd created. There were no signs of wear on the rope and the ax hadn't budged and everything else was working just as it should, too. It seemed like her training and preparation had done its job. She continued to pull, only taking quick glances over toward him while he scrambled out of the crevasse, using her leverage and his ax to help him inch his way to solid ground. Soon his entire waist was visible, then his knees, and in a few moments he had crawled over to where she was anchored. It had only been maybe thirty seconds since he'd fallen, but it felt much, much longer to her.

Val's muscles ached, but she didn't let up her grip on the rope until Jonah was beside her, clearly safe, and the rope hung loosely against the ax. "I'm okay," he gasped.

It was only then, when he was right there and she heard those words, that she was sure he was truly safe. She allowed her fingers to slowly unclench and let the rope fall. She slumped forward, feeling totally drained.

The adrenaline that had pushed her through the ordeal evaporated as quickly as it had come, leaving her exhausted and unable to move, trying to breathe in air that was so thin she needed to force her brain to not panic. She closed her eyes, wrapped her arms around her legs, rested her head on her knees and forced her breaths to slow. She was fine. Jonah was safe. She repeated it to herself like a mantra, using it to calm the storm inside her.

"That's a familiar sight," Jonah said, his voice,

strong and right beside her, soothing her more than her own words possibly could.

Val was so focused on the sound of him speaking that it took a few seconds for her to register what he'd said, and then a few more to understand it. When she realized she was in the same position she'd been in when they'd first met on Mt. Si—out of breath and exhausted, curled in a ball, on the side of a mountain—she chuckled. "Got a granola bar to share, by any chance?" she asked, remembering the snack that had gotten her to uncurl back then. She turned her head enough so she could see his reaction.

And she was rewarded when a wide grin spread across his face, followed by a loud laugh. A real, warm, rolling, relieved laugh. The sound of it coursed through her, flooding her with joy. That laugh had stuck with her since that day last year, and it was just as wonderful as she remembered. She reached toward him with one gloved hand, and he immediately clasped it tightly in his own. She smiled and laughed with him, feeding off his amusement until she was shaking with it.

They stayed in that position, both laughing so hard they were gasping, for a long minute before settling into a silence only occasionally broken by a lingering giggle. Once she could breathe again, she knew they should get up and go meet the rangers, but she simply couldn't force herself to move. She was tired to her very bones, and being there with her hand in his was all she wanted. She looked over to see the rangers walking their way, anyway, so she didn't try to force herself to do anything quite yet.

"You saved me," he said, his eyes capturing hers. "Thanks."

She fell into them, wishing she could stay there forever. She knew she couldn't, but that didn't stop her from enjoying this moment for all it was worth.

She smiled and squeezed his hand. "Of course. I need someone to corroborate my crazy mountain lion story when the rangers get here," she said, nodding toward the men who were on their way.

Jonah laughed again but didn't let himself get carried away with it. "Yeah, nobody would believe you without a second witness. And bonus, now you're a hero who saves people on the sides of mountains," he said.

"It happens more than you might think," she said, starting to giggle.

Soon they were both laughing uncontrollably again, all of their relief and exhaustion and more feelings Val didn't want to try to identify overflowing. She wasn't sure when her laughter turned to tears, but soon he was sitting beside her with his arms wrapped around her as she cried yet again.

"I can't believe I'm crying again," she said into his shoulder, unable to stop the tears from coming down.

"Did you let yourself cry at all since you found out?" he asked.

She shook her head. "I wanted to be brave," she told him.

"You can be brave and accept what happened and trust in God and still cry sometimes," he said softly, wiping a tear off her cheek with the pad of his thumb. "It's been stored up for a long while now, and being out here has helped you finally let it out."

She knew it wasn't Mt. Rainier that helped her but being with him. Someone she trusted so completely, someone she felt so very safe with. The tears slowed and stopped, and then she smiled. She felt better. Lighter. As if all the emotions she hadn't expressed when she'd gotten her diagnosis had been weighing her down all this time and she had finally set them free.

She looked up at Jonah, who was still hugging her.

"I've cried more on this mountain than I ever have in my life," she told him with a quivery laugh.

Jonah smiled. "I think maybe that's what you needed," he said.

She nodded and tucked herself against him again. *Just one more minute of this, God, please. I'll be able to make it on my own if I can have another minute.*

She listened to his breath as he held her and felt her heart swell. And she was happy.

Then Val heard the crunching sounds of footsteps. She and Jonah both shifted, looking toward the sound. The rangers had gotten to them, two men wearing jackets with state park logos on them and holding a red stretcher.

"Should've asked for more than a minute," she mumbled to herself.

"What?" Jonah asked.

"Never mind. The rangers are here." She didn't need to say that their time was up. She was sure he already knew.

She shifted away from him, immediately wanting to curl back up and stay there, but knowing that wasn't an option. She began to gather the supplies she had scattered around herself during the rescue and got her gear set to rights before standing up to greet them. Jonah was still sitting and waved at them from where he was, but Val didn't have time to wonder why before she turned her attention to the rescue team.

The rangers got right down to business. "Are you okay? Either of you injured?" one of them asked.

Val was about to respond that they were fine and wouldn't need that stretcher to get to the helicopter when Jonah said, "I twisted my ankle pretty badly falling into a crevasse. Val got me out, or it could've been much worse. I don't think it's broken but can't be sure. I'll need help the rest of the way."

The men nodded, looking impressed. "We saw. You know your stuff," one of them commented.

But Val's attention was entirely on Jonah. "You're hurt? Why didn't you tell me?"

He shrugged, though he did look a little contrite at upsetting her. "It's not that bad, and I didn't want you to start worrying. I was going to bring it up before we started hiking again, I promise," he said, holding up his hands as if to show he was being sincere.

While she'd laughed and cried and they had hugged, he had been in pain and saying nothing about it. She wanted to be mad at him for keeping quiet, but she couldn't be anything but grateful for that short blissful time they had spent since she'd rescued him. If she'd known he was injured, none of that would've happened and they both knew it.

But now that time was over and they needed to face the realities around them, including his injury.

One of the men bent to examine Jonah's ankle. Val watched as he wrapped it in tape. "We'll get you onto the stretcher and then the helicopter will take you to the hospital," one said before turning to his radio and talking to the pilot.

"There's a cougar!" Val burst out, remembering

the poor animal that needed help, which she had forgotten in the recent excitement. "We need to tell you about the mountain lion we saw near Disappointment Cleaver!"

The rangers looked at each other and then back at her. "You can't possibly be talking about a mountain lion at this elevation," one of them said, shaking his head in disbelief.

Val wasn't all that surprised. After all, it sounded crazy to her, too, and she'd actually seen it. Luckily, she had Jonah there to corroborate her story. "There really is a mountain lion," he told them. "I saved the coordinates on my GPS. It's probably been through all our beef jerky by this point and is searching for something else to eat. And it's definitely injured," he added. Val nodded in agreement.

The rangers still seemed skeptical, but she and Jonah relayed all the information they had to the men. When they finished their explanation, one of the rangers shook his head. "Are you absolutely sure it was a mountain lion? That sounds impossible," he said.

Val and Jonah both nodded. "We really saw it. Definitely a mountain lion, and injured, and needs help," Val said with emphasis, hoping they were convincing enough that these men would get someone up there searching for it as soon as possible.

"It needs immediate medical attention," Jonah said, clearly thinking the same thing.

The men still seemed to be in disbelief, even after all that, but one of them grabbed his radio and called in the information. After reassuring the person on the other end that he was serious, that there was a report of a large wild animal in need of assistance up on Ingraham Flats, and giving all the information Val and Jonah had to help them find the animal, he turned back to them.

"They'll need the helicopter to go look for it. We can still take you to the hospital, if you think your ankle is broken," one of them said to Jonah, "but we'd be able to get to the animal much faster if we could drop you at Camp Muir, where a medical staffer can take a look."

Val wasn't at all surprised to see Jonah nodding. "Camp Muir will be fine," he told them.

Val watched him to be sure he truly was okay and wasn't just saying that, but the smile he gave her reassured her and they all started off toward the helicopter, Jonah strapped to the stretcher as a precaution.

In no time, they were all in the helicopter, her sitting, Jonah still on the stretcher. They had headphones on so they could hear each other, but Val didn't feel the need to speak. She didn't want to talk to Jonah or anybody else right now. There was nothing left to say, was there?

And she was worn down and ready for a very long rest. She looked at Jonah and he gave her an encouraging little smile, and she smiled back as best she could.

Jonah watched Val for a few more seconds before resting his head on the stretcher and feeling the change in gravity as the helicopter took off. "There were no signs of a crevasse before you stepped on it, huh?" one of the rangers asked into the headphones, sounding like Jonah must've been the victim of random bad luck.

Jonah felt a little embarrassed, but he told the truth. "I don't know, actually. I wasn't really watching where I was going at the time."

The two rangers looked at one another, and Jonah agreed with what their expressions said. His attention had wandered, and that was dangerous. He knew that as well as anyone.

But he wasn't exactly surprised at himself, what with Val's unexpected revelation. He was amazed he had managed to stop himself from falling all the way in once he had dropped to the ground, actually. He'd been so stunned he might've hardly noticed what had happened until he was hitting bottom.

Val had cancer. This bright, strong, clever woman, who had already been through so much, was carrying a burden of that magnitude, as well, and seemed to be doing it all on her own. And yet she'd spent so much of the hike attempting to help him with his hurt. Instead of feeling scared and alone, she was full of life and determination, concern and kindness.

So he'd been staring at her instead of watching his feet, and that's when he'd fallen into a hole in the ground that might or might not have been obvious, he really had no idea.

He didn't know what he could say to her about what she'd told him. He had so many feelings about it, and yet he couldn't figure out how to turn any of them into sentences. Even if he knew exactly what to say, this definitely wasn't the time. Not with the rangers and the helicopter pilot all listening in.

But he wanted to talk to her, to say words and hear her replies, about anything, about everything. Even when he'd been injured, lying in the snow, exhausted and overwhelmed by all that had happened that day, she'd been able to make him laugh, and he had almost forgotten what it was like to laugh. He wanted more of that time, just the two of them.

For now, though, he would just lie on the stretcher as the helicopter flew them back to Camp Muir, since there seemed to be little option in the matter. They would talk there. He would think of what to say, and when they got there, he would pull her aside and say it.

The voice of the ranger cut into his thoughts once again. "So, a whiteout, a mountain lion, a crevasse, and an injured ankle, huh? Sounds like a summit attempt for the record books," the man said.

Jonah couldn't help but smirk. "It really was," he answered. *More than you could possibly know*, he added silently.

Jonah looked over at where Val was sitting. She was leaning back, her eyes closed, apparently lost in her own world. He took a deep breath. They would talk at the camp, he assured himself. He'd know what to say by then.

Val had been unhappy when the rangers had first walked up, had felt like they were intruding into her time with Jonah, but now she was glad for their intervention. Firstly because Jonah was injured and they could get him medical help, and secondly because it made it impossible for her and Jonah to discuss what she'd told him.

Val felt a deep foreboding about what would happen now that Jonah knew about her diagnosis. It had been a long, difficult hike and she'd finally caved and shared that information. Even though it felt right in so many ways to tell him—and his strength buoyed her in a way she could hardly understand—she was very aware that now it was going to be even harder to say goodbye to him at Camp Muir.

If he had believed she just wasn't interested for her own reasons when they parted ways at the bottom of the mountain, he'd have let her go without a fight. She was sure of that. But now that he knew the whole story, she could already see that he was ready to be the hero, to save her. He was a firefighter and a pastor. Saving people was his instinct, his approach to the world.

But this wasn't something he could save her from, and in the process he would just hurt himself. She'd read enough about chemo to know the path ahead wasn't going to be easy for anybody involved, and she couldn't let him put himself into that situation. So she would need to be strong enough to push him away, even though all she wanted was to hold him close.

She listened to the sound of the helicopter's blades, muffled through her headphones, trying to relax and allow her body to recover as they got closer and closer to Camp Muir. And in what felt like a ridiculously short time compared to the long hike up, they were touching down right near where everything had started.

"You were so close to making it to the summit," one of the rangers said through the headphones as they landed. "Better luck next time."

Val didn't respond, just took off her headphones and climbed out, getting out of the way so Jonah could be brought out on the stretcher. The rangers began to haul Jonah out of the helicopter as a small crowd formed near Camp Muir. Val guessed it wasn't every day they saw something like this.

And then a woman with a medical kit broke from the group and ran over to them, talking to Jonah and the rangers. Val was just a little too far away to hear what they were saying over the sound of the helicopter, but was relieved to see the woman study Jonah's ankle for a minute and not appear all that worried. In a moment, Jonah was free of the stretcher and standing beside the woman, shaking hands with the rangers who had helped them. Then the two men came over to Val and she shook their hands as well, and they hopped back into the helicopter.

Val walked over to Jonah and the woman. "I told them I could make it from here okay and that they should head out to look for the mountain lion," he said. "I just need a couple shoulders to lean on and I'll be fine."

Val was happy to lend a shoulder, and soon the three of them were making their way slowly toward

Camp Muir. Val was aware of every part of her body that was touching Jonah's and felt a deep ache inside. She knew a part of her heart, a piece of her puzzle, would be missing forever if she didn't see him again. But it was the best gift she could give him, not allowing him to add another burden to his shoulders. So she would do what she needed to do.

"I'm Yolanda, by the way," the woman said with a little wave from her free hand. "We'll get you both inside the building and checked out."

"I'm okay—" Val started to protest.

Jonah gave her a little look. "You had hypothermia not too long ago, Val," he reminded her.

In all the craziness of the day, she'd forgotten that. "Alright, but your ankle is the important thing. I really do feel perfectly fine," she reassured Yolanda.

"Well, I'm so glad you're safe," a voice said near Val's shoulder. She looked up, surprised to see Keith standing there. He must have seen them land and walked up while she was focused on helping Jonah and talking to Yolanda.

"Thank you" was all she could think of to say.

"We needed to turn around because of the whiteout. Looks like you two got stranded out there, huh? Bad luck your friend got injured," he said, not sounding all that sorry about Jonah's ankle. "Since we're all done early, you and I can spend a little time to-gether now," he continued.

"Jonah needs medical attention," Val told him, knowing she sounded a little irritated. She couldn't help it.

Keith smiled at her, not appearing to hear any-thing off about her response. It seemed that this guy did not take hints well. She caught Jonah's eye and they had a silent conversation that went something like:

Do you believe this guy?

I know, right?

Totally oblivious.

They both bit back smiles as Keith continued his ill-fated attempt to convince Val to like him.

"We should go for a hike together sometime, you know. Have you ever done the Wonderland Trail?"

She shook her head, but before she could manage a single word, he started in again. "It's absolutely beautiful and will be the best week of your life. We could make that happen a couple weeks from now, before the end of the season. What do you think?"

Val was thinking quite a few things, in fact. She thought that spending a week hiking around Mt. Rainier sounded fantastic. And she thought that at-tempting it with Keith would make it the most miserable week of her life. She knew exactly who she would want with her on that one.

Please, God, someday, she prayed.

"Come on, Val, what do you think?" Keith asked again, his voice wheedling.

"I'm not interested," she said, doubting he would get the message but trying anyway.

"I guess it's hard to get an entire week off work. I run my own company, so I can make my own hours, but most people aren't that lucky, I know. Well, how about we go one weekend for a day hike? There are a ton of them around here."

It was time to be more direct, and she wanted to do it before they walked up to the rest of the crowd just a few yards away. She thought through her options, trying to decide how best to be both tactful and clear. From what she'd seen thus far, she would need to be *very* clear.

"No, I am not interested, Keith," she said, rolling her eyes at her inability to come up with anything better than that.

"Oh, come on!" he said, putting his hand on her arm.

That was it. Val knew this was not appropriate behavior and she would need to say something about it. Just as she opened her mouth to say something that was sure to make things very awkward, though, Jonah spoke up beside her.

"Not okay, man," he said, his voice calm and steady. The look on his face definitely fell under the category *Not Amused*.

"What?" Keith asked, looking confused.

"Val has tried to make it clear that she's not interested and you keep pushing. It's time to give up," Jonah told him matter-of-factly.

Val looked Keith straight in the eye and nodded her agreement, and after a confused moment, Keith took his hand off Val's arm.

"Thank you," she said to him, and he gave her an embarrassed little nod. To Jonah, she didn't need to say any words. A glance said plenty, and a quick upturn of his lips was enough to show that he'd gotten the message.

It had been a very long time since anybody had done something like that for her. Even when she'd been engaged, she'd always been the only one willing to stand up for her. Brian had never managed to even notice what was going on, let alone find the energy to say something about it.

And she could stand up for herself and did it plenty. Still, it was nice to have the weight off her shoulders a little, even if it was just for today. It made her feel a bit less lonely.

* * *

Jonah was relieved to see that Val hadn't minded his interference. He couldn't help it. As soon as Keith had touched her, every alarm had gone off inside him and he'd spoken before he could stop himself.

"Sorry," Keith mumbled to Val, looking very uncomfortable.

Val gave him a little smile. "That's okay. Best of luck and God bless," she told him. It was a kind dismissal, but a dismissal nonetheless, and he finally seemed to take a hint and separate from their group.

Jonah was impressed with Val's behavior toward Keith. There was no visible anger in Val, no grudge against the man for his behavior. Only kindness and care. Jonah knew he'd been like that, too, able to forgive easily, before Becca's death. He hoped he still was. *God, help me be like her.*

"Thanks," Val said to Jonah as they continued toward the hut.

"You're welcome," he answered. "Not that I didn't think you could handle it yourself or anything. He just shouldn't have done that, and I couldn't help it."

"I imagine that happened a few times to Becca, too, huh?"

Jonah laughed at the memories that flooded him. "She had this crazy knack to turn any problem into a joke, so whenever a guy got too close for her comfort, she would shut him down in such a way that would leave them both laughing. I don't know how she did that."

Val laughed. "I wish I had that ability. Sometimes I let my mouth run away with me and say things in a way that is unkind."

Jonah shook his head but didn't say anything. He couldn't imagine Val saying anything unkind. Even if she did, he was sure the sparkle in her eyes would keep it from being too harsh. She was a woman of faith, and that gave her a strength and calm and loving demeanor that didn't seem like it could possibly be offensive.

He thought about Becca and her remarkable ability to defuse any situation. He was sure she and Val would have gotten along well, and he wished they could have had the chance to meet. He was glad Val didn't mind him talking about Becca, because it felt good to share. It hurt, too, so much that every time he started he wasn't sure his heart could take it, but the weight that lifted off him as he talked was something he'd never expected.

Val was right about carrying Becca in his heart; he'd been trying to run away from her for weeks, but that just made everything worse, because he couldn't run from her or from what happened. She would always be there with him, and ignoring her would never make him happy.

Val was right about a lot of things, but he didn't believe she was right about them not being together because of her diagnosis, and he knew he would need to say something. They were approaching all the people at Camp Muir and had probably put Yolanda through enough awkwardness already, but he would find his moment.

"You both had some close calls out there," Yolanda commented, breaking into his thoughts.

"We really did," Jonah answered, glancing over at Val.

"I'll remember it always," she told him.

The words were sweet but also had a sense of finality Jonah didn't like to hear. She knew he wasn't going to abandon her just because she had cancer, right? He was certain she knew him well enough at this point to not think that of him, but perhaps he needed to reassure her, to show her that he would stick with her through it all. He vowed to do so the minute they had time to speak privately.

God, I trust You to tell me what to say and when to say it, he prayed.

He noticed that it didn't hurt him to talk to God anymore. It was like there had been a wall there and now it was gone and he could pray again. Even if Val refused him and he never saw her again, she had given him so much in these few short hours. Things were still far from perfect, and he was still broken in many ways, but he had his faith back, and that was more than he could've asked for from a day on a mountain.

The people in front of them shifted so Jonah, Val and Yolanda could get into the building. Before they could cross the doorway, though, two people called out to Val and pushed through the others to give her an awkward hug, since she still had Jonah's arm around her shoulders. Val's face lit up, and Jonah recognized one of the pair as Clay Williams, his hiking buddy from a couple years ago. So the other one must be Ellie, and it was obvious why Val had started grinning so broadly when she'd seen them.

They were standing so close to one another, hands locked together, with an aura of pure joy that was obviously about more than seeing their friend again. It seemed Val's hope that they would tell each other how they felt had come to pass. They looked like two people who were deeply in love.

Jonah shifted his weight so Val could move out from beneath his arm, though he missed her closeness. She dropped her backpack and properly hugged her two friends with all the force and vitality she somehow managed to muster even after such an exhausting day. She seemed blissfully happy at the change in them, and they seemed relieved that she was back safe. He watched the reunion with a smile on his lips.

After a few moments, Clay noticed Jonah for the first time and recognition flitted across his face. "Jonah, you're the one Val was hiking with?" he asked, smiling and holding out a hand toward him.

Jonah nodded. "Yeah, and it was a good thing, too," he said, giving an awkward handshake while trying to balance on one foot. "She did a great job keeping me alive."

"We need to get you seated inside," Yolanda said, gesturing toward the door.

Val moved back to Jonah's side and pulled his arm around her shoulders again, and they stepped inside the building, with Clay and Ellie trailing them. They stood by the door for a few seconds to allow their eyes to adjust to the dim interior after being out in the bright sunshine. "Seems like you two have quite the story to tell," Clay prompted as the group hobbled over to the nearest bunk.

"Oh, nothing all that exciting," Val said, a hint of mischief in her voice that tickled Jonah.

"Just a whiteout at Disappointment Cleaver," Jonah added casually as he sat down, careful not to jolt his ankle.

"An earthquake before that," Val reminded him.

"Right. And then there was some hypothermia," he continued.

"Only a little. Of course there was the mountain lion, too," she said, as if all of this was just a normal series of events.

"And then the crevasse and a busted ankle and a helicopter ride. That about it?" he asked her.

Val nodded, sitting down beside him. "I think so. And some gorgeous views, of course."

They giggled at themselves as her friends tried to absorb everything they'd just said.

"You have to be making this up. There is no way you saw a mountain lion out there," Ellie said, shaking her head in the same way the rangers had when they'd heard the story.

Jonah guessed that would be the reaction pretty much everyone would have if he tried to explain to them about this hike up Mt. Rainier. The only person he could imagine not questioning his sanity or honesty would be Becca. Partly because she knew him well enough that she believed and trusted him implicitly, and partly because she'd have had no idea how strange a thing it was to see a mountain lion that high up.

The thoughts of his sister ached, but not in that terrible way from before. In a way that felt healthy, healing. The vise around his heart had broken, and it was nothing less than a miracle. And he had Val to thank for it. Her and God and her faith in Him.

Yolanda's radio crackled to life, and after a few seconds of listening, she turned to the group. "I wouldn't have believed it myself, but they said they found the mountain lion near the GPS coordinates you provided. It's been tranquilized and a helicopter is evacuating it to a wild animal medical facility."

"So they're taking it to the vet," Val said, a feeling of relief washing through her.

Yolanda gave a little chuckle. "Pretty much, yeah. The vet will evaluate the animal and see if it can recuperate and be released back into the wild."

"I'll pray for that," she said.

"So will I," Jonah added, giving her a little smile.

It warmed her heart to think of Jonah praying about anything, but especially about the animal they had met together on the mountain.

Val felt a wave of warmth and calm course through her. Jonah was going to be fine—she just knew it. He had found God again and he would smile again and laugh again, and that made her heart fill to bursting. Even if she wasn't in his life, he would go on and recover from his losses and find strength in God.

Only after hearing about the mountain lion's fate from Yolanda did Ellie and Clay manage to accept it as truth, and she couldn't blame them. "Wow, you had quite an adventure," Clay said to her.

"We really did," she said, looking at Jonah.

He smiled and she felt her heart soar before it plummeted once again. No, no, no. She couldn't allow herself to dream.

Luckily, Yolanda interrupted her. "You were hypothermic on the mountain?" she asked Val, kneeling in front of her and shining a light into each of her eyes.

Val nodded. "But Jonah helped me get warm and there doesn't seem to be any frostbite or lasting issues," she added.

Yolanda nodded, but she still checked Val's temperature and blood pressure and examined her fingers and toes. Then she asked Val to name the president, what year it was, and other checks that her mental faculties were up and running.

"You seem perfectly healthy," Yolanda concluded at last.

Val knew she wasn't actually *perfectly* healthy but didn't feel the need to share that information with this woman she had only just met. She looked up at her friends who were standing nearby waiting for her. She would need to tell them, though.

"I'm going to go grab a few more things, and then, Jonah, you'll need to lie down on the bunk so I can look at that ankle," Yolanda said, standing and walking to the other end of the room.

Val knew it was time for her to leave and let Yolanda check Jonah, but she wasn't quite ready to go yet. She looked up at her friends. "I'll meet you guys outside in a minute?" she asked.

They seemed to take the hint and scooted out the door.

The moment wasn't completely private. Yolanda was right there on the other side of the building, and people were coming in and out as they prepared to leave Mt. Rainier, but Val knew this might be her last chance to say goodbye. She tried, but the words weren't coming, and Yolanda was back in a flash. Val stood so Jonah would have space to stretch out on the bunk.

"Will you come back in after the exam? We need to talk," Jonah said, his eyes locked on hers.

Part of Val warned her to stop this now, to say goodbye and run, but she couldn't. Not yet. So she nodded and walked out the door with a little wave, and for the first time since they left that morning, they were separated. Their hike was over.

Outside in the bright sunshine, Val reunited with her friends. "So what's happened around here since

I left this morning?" she asked, glancing at the two, who had their arms wrapped around each other. "It seems like I wasn't the only one with an exciting morning."

Clay and Ellie filled Val in on all the details, and while her heart was incredibly happy for them, it also ached. She was so close to having the same thing herself, but instead of leaving with the person she loved, she would need to say goodbye and walk away. She didn't know if she'd have the strength to do it.

"Val?" said Ellie, cutting into her thoughts. "Do you need to sit down or something? You look pale."

Val turned back to her friends and attempted a smile. "I'm sorry. I'm just distracted. I need to go check on Jonah—" She couldn't manage the words *say goodbye to Jonah*—it was too heartbreaking. "And then we can all get out of here," she finished.

Her friends nodded, though they still looked concerned, and Val prepared herself for what needed to happen next.

Jonah had watched Val leave, every bit of him wanting to call her back. It felt like a piece of himself was walking out that door, and he was afraid he'd never get it back. Everything told him that he belonged by Val's side, and that he needed to return to that spot as soon as possible. It was difficult to concentrate on what was going on as Yolanda checked his eyes, blood pressure and temperature.

Jonah wanted to be out there with Val, but he knew that wasn't an option and that she'd come back like she'd said she would, so with a conscious effort he managed to turn his attention to the medic. He needed to finish this so he could see Val again.

"Your vital signs are all good. How's the ankle feeling?" Yolanda asked as she carefully began unwrapping the bandage the ranger had put on for him.

Jonah hadn't really thought about his ankle all that much and took a moment to assess. He'd had plenty of injuries along the way, so he was pretty sure he knew what it would feel like if it was broken. It wasn't nearly that bad, which was a relief. "It throbs, but I don't think I broke it," he told her.

He grimaced a little as she started to poke and prod, but his eyes and mind kept wandering to the door. Val was probably getting caught up with her friends—he just wished he could see her and hear her voice. Those hours on the mountain hadn't been enough. He suspected an entire lifetime wouldn't be enough.

Yolanda finished her examination and began rewrapping his ankle, adding a cold pack into the wrappings to help the swelling. "It does seem like just a minor sprain, but you might want to get X-rays to be sure it's nothing more serious. Keep it elevated and rest it for a few days. A couple of rangers will be back to help you down to the parking lot with a stretcher, and we can call an ambulance if you like."

Jonah shook his head. "I'll be fine, thanks. I don't think I need a stretcher. I could have a few friends—"

"It's a necessary precaution," Yolanda said, cutting off any argument Jonah was going to make.

Jonah nodded, and Yolanda put a call through on her radio and listened for a minute before turning her attention back to him. "It'll be a bit before anyone can help you out of here, so in the meantime just relax and don't get up," she said, giving him a look that showed she meant it.

He gave her a thumbs-up. "Stay here and rest. Got it," he said, even though he wanted to leave as soon as possible.

But he would listen to the medic and trust that Val would come back. So after the woman propped his foot up on top of his bag and left, Jonah laced his fingers across his chest and waited.

Luckily, he didn't need to wait very long. Less than a minute later, Val's silhouette appeared in the doorway and he felt his heart thump heavily in his chest. He smiled at her, but because of the sunlight streaming in behind her, he couldn't see her expression.

It was only when she came closer that he could

see how serious she looked. He wondered if something had happened with her friends.

"What did she say?" Val asked, gesturing to his ankle.

"Said it looks like a minor sprain. Keep it elevated and stay off it a day or two and it should be fine. I'll need to wait a little bit for the rangers to help me down to my car, and she said I need to be taken out on a stretcher again as a 'necessary precaution,' but that's all," he explained, hoping to reassure her.

She did look relieved, though still worried. She moved her hand as if to rest it on his arm, then seemed to think better of it and let it fall back to her side. "You don't need to get X-rays?"

Jonah shook his head. "If it gets worse I will, but I don't think it'll be necessary."

"That's good," she said, but her look didn't change.

Anxiety started to mount inside him as the reasons for her mood dwindled. "Is everything okay with Ellie and Clay?" he asked, almost hoping that was the problem.

Val nodded, giving him a little smile that didn't reach her eyes. "They finally shared how they feel, and it seems like that conversation went very well. They have their first official date set up for tomorrow night. I expect to be getting a wedding invitation in the next few months," she finished with a little laugh.

So if that wasn't what was worrying her, what was? Jonah racked his brain trying to come up with some reason that made sense, besides the one that he feared.

Before he could come up with anything, she started speaking again. "Listen, Jonah, I think it's best if we say goodbye here and just leave it at that," she said, wiping away a tear that started to roll down her cheek.

Jonah felt as if the ice pack was on his chest instead of his ankle, and as if it weighed a hundred pounds. It was what he'd been afraid of, but he couldn't quite believe it. "You do?" he asked.

"I do. I just don't think this will work," she said softly.

Did she think he wouldn't do everything he could to help her as she battled cancer? That made no sense to him. "But I'm not afraid—" he began.

"No, Jonah," she said firmly, cutting him off, not allowing any discussion.

He tried to wrap his mind around what she was saying and couldn't quite manage it. The two of them were going to be spending the rest of their lives with each other, right? Clay and Ellie would be getting an invitation to their wedding, wouldn't they?

"I think it's for the best," she repeated, sounding resolute.

It was only when she said that they wouldn't be together that he realized he had already begun planning an entire life with Val by his side. He felt to his core that they belonged together. But here she was saying that wouldn't happen.

"You have enough on your plate without adding a cancer diagnosis to it. If I get over this and healthy again, I will call you, I promise."

He looked in her eyes and could see how hard all of this was for her to say. And that she wanted no arguments from him. He didn't want to agree with her, but he also didn't want to make this any harder for her than it already was.

"Okay," he answered, pushing down his arguments and reasoning for now.

She nodded a thanks and walked quickly away. Jonah could tell she was crying as she did so.

He wanted to jump up and follow her, regardless of his ankle or anything else, tell her it was a mistake, that they'd be together and make it through all this. But he'd already told himself not to make it any harder on her, so he stayed where he was and watched her leave.

Chapter Eight

Val dropped to the ground just outside the little hut and buried her head in her knees, trying to take deep breaths. It was for the best, she told herself. It was for the best. God would help them both through this and they would be together when she was healthy.

Suddenly extremely tired, the walk to her car seemed much too long, an impossible task she couldn't imagine accomplishing after the day she'd had. She just wanted to go to sleep for a few weeks. But before she could curl up and hide in bed, she'd need to get to her car. And she had an appointment at the hospital in two days. So she promised herself a shower and a cry and a good night's sleep. She took a deep breath, willing herself to unfurl and stand up.

"What's going on, Val?" Ellie said from above her, sounding worried.

Looking up, she saw her friends kneeling beside her, clearly concerned. "Is something wrong with Jonah?" Clay asked.

Val shook her head. "He'll be fine. It's just a sprain," she said.

"So why are you upset? You can talk to us," Ellie said. Clay nodded encouragingly. "What happened in there?"

"It's hard to say goodbye, that's all," Val said.

"But it's not really goodbye, right? He obviously likes you. Anyone can see that," Ellie said.

Val managed to hold back the wave of tears that threatened. "It's really goodbye," she said. "Clay, if he contacts you about me, tell him I told you not to give him my number or pass on messages."

Clay looked even more confused than he already had, but he nodded.

"Now I want to get off this mountain," she told them.

Ellie looked as if she was going to argue with Val, demand more details. "I'll tell you what's going on, I promise," Val reassured her friends. "But I need to leave now."

Val was relieved to see Ellie process what she was saying and give a nod. They all gathered their gear, which was luckily right there. Val didn't want to even think about going into that little building again or wait while her friends did, because she wasn't sure she'd be able to stick to her resolve. She needed to get some distance between her and Jonah as soon as possible.

In just a few seconds, everyone was ready and they started the hike back to the car. Val turned her attention to her friends. Clay was carrying Ellie's bag, but besides that little acknowledgment of her recent illness, Ellie looked as healthy as ever. "You seem so much better than you did a few hours ago," Val told her friend, happy to have a topic of discussion that veered far away from Jonah.

Ellie rolled her eyes. "Yeah, I was mostly fine by dawn, actually. It was just a weird bug, I guess."

Clay took her hand. "You should still take it easy, though."

She gave him such a sweet smile that Val's heart gave a big, hard tug. "I'm glad you two talked while I was gone," she told them.

"We are, too," Ellie said softly. She and Clay looked at each other as if they'd only just seen each other for the first time.

It was so very sweet, and Val stayed silent, not wanting to intrude on their private moment. Her friends were happy and that was wonderful.

After a short time, they turned their attention back to her. "So what happened with Jonah? Something big, clearly, and you need to talk about it."

Val shrugged. "It doesn't matter what happened between us. The fact is that we can't be together, and it's better if we don't see each other."

"Why?" Ellie asked.

Val knew she had hidden her diagnosis from her friends long enough. Now that they were nearly down the mountain, it was time to tell them everything.

"There's something you should know," she said, taking a deep breath and then letting everything out in a rush. "I have stage three breast cancer. I found out a couple of weeks ago and I didn't want to tell you because I knew you'd worry and wouldn't want to attempt Rainier and I *had* to try to summit. But I didn't make it and I can't put Jonah through all that and I just want to go home."

Clay and Ellie stared at her, stunned, but Val didn't stop walking and soon they were rushing to catch up to her as she crossed the parking lot to Ellie's car, which they'd used to carpool there. "I can't..." Ellie said, her words trailing off to nothing.

Val couldn't blame her. That was a lot of information in thirty seconds. "I'm doing okay," she told them. "I'm starting chemotherapy in a couple of days, and if that goes well, I'll contact Jonah when I'm healthy again. I can't be a burden in his life, but we can try to be together when it's all over."

She knew she was saying this more to herself than

to them, but it felt good to say that hope out loud, as if giving voice to it made it more likely to come true.

Clay and Ellie exchanged a glance, but Val didn't even attempt to read it. She was way too tired. The three of them shoved their bags into the back, and Val slid gratefully into the back seat, closing her eyes and leaning her forehead against the cold window. Now to rest and relax and attempt to forget the unforgettable.

Ellie started the engine and drove out of the parking lot, and Val was asleep before they hit the highway.

Jonah looked at his phone. He was itching to message Clay to ask him for help. Jonah would need to get in contact with Val somehow so they could talk about her feelings and he could reassure her that he wanted to be with her. He wasn't going to give up on her that easy, that was for sure.

But he'd wait a little bit first. He'd be patient.

Two more rangers walked into Camp Muir carrying another big stretcher. "Are you ready to get off this mountain?" one of them asked Jonah.

Jonah guessed the men they'd met at the summit were still busy with the mountain lion and was thankful there were others around to help so he wouldn't be stuck lying here for who knew how long. Now that Val had left, there was no reason to stick around. Quickly and efficiently, they got him settled on the stretcher and prepared for the long walk down to his car.

When they left the building and came back out into the bright sunshine, Jonah looked around for Val and her friends, but it was clear they'd gotten out of there quickly and efficiently themselves, because none of them were anywhere in sight. Val was gone, but Jonah was confident that, with God's— and Clay's—help, he would see her again. He had so many things to tell her.

The rangers walked carefully, trying not to jostle Jonah too much as they carried his weight between them, but even so it didn't take long to get to Jonah's car. They had clearly done this many times before, and Jonah hoped this was the only time he'd need to be the one on that stretcher. When they arrived at his vehicle, the two rangers unstrapped him and set down Jonah's pack. Jonah stood and leaned against his car door, thanking them and assuring them that he didn't need any more help. As soon as the men were heading back the way they'd come, Jonah began scouring the area for Val or her car. There weren't many vehicles left in the lot, and it only took a few seconds to confirm that she was already gone.

But he would contact Clay and he could talk to Val, so there was still hope, he told himself. In fact, it was probably better to give her a little time, even though he desperately wanted to see her again. Hug her again. Kiss her again.

His phone dinged in his pocket, and he pulled it out. It was from Clay. He smiled at the fortuitous timing, until he actually read what Clay had written.

Hey Jonah. Val asked me not to give you her number or pass along messages, so please don't ask me to do those things.

Jonah struggled to accept what he was reading. It felt as if all the muscles in his body were about to give way. So that was it, the only way he knew to contact her, and she'd already cut that off, leaving him alone and bewildered. He didn't know what to do next.

He slumped into the driver's seat and closed his eyes. Was that really it? He was just supposed to go on with his life?

A sense of calm came over him. He knew what to do. Jonah leaned forward against his steering wheel. He began to pray.

"God, help me choose the right path. I trust You. Please let me know what I should do," he whispered. Then he thought for a moment and added, "And thank You. For Becca, for Val, for every second I've had with each of them. Thank You."

He finished and kept his eyes closed. He felt

lighter, as if a burden was no longer weighing him down. He'd be able to manage anything, as long as he kept God in his heart and continued to pray.

His phone dinged again and he glanced at it once more. A little smile crossed his lips as he read the new message.

Val parked her car in the busy parking lot and looked up at the large glass building. She had prepared for her first chemotherapy appointment, but now that it was here, she was nervous. She said a little prayer and opened the car door, grabbing her purse. Before she could stand, she glanced at her phone and saw a text from Ellie.

Clay and I are thinking about you. Let us know if you need us to come sit with you and we'll be there. Love you!

She messaged back that she would be fine and she would see them that evening. Her friends had wanted to come with her but had both already had plans that day. They had assured her they could come if she needed them, but she didn't want to make them do that if she didn't have to. She could do this on her own.

One last look up at the building, a quick prayer for strength, and she was walking up to the big sliding doors. The day was hot, but inside was chilly, and Val was considering going back to her car for her sweater when she stopped walking and stared. There, standing just a few feet inside the door was Jonah. He gave her a little wave. "Hi, Val," he said.

"Jonah?" Even with him standing right there in front of her, she couldn't manage to process the information. He couldn't be *here*.

"Are you ready for your appointment?" he asked. "I brought a few different things for us to do to kill time. How do you feel about crossword puzzles? Or Sudoku? I've got lots of options," he said, gesturing to a hefty cloth bag hanging from his shoulder.

She could hardly comprehend what was happening. "What are you doing here?" she asked.

"I want to be here, with you. Through all this."

No. She couldn't let him. "Jonah, you don't need—"

"I do, though," he said, cutting off her argument before she could start. "I need *you*, Val. I need you in my life. This doesn't scare me," he said, gesturing to the hospital around them. "What scares me is missing out on any time I can have with you."

Val stood there, letting that sink in. She didn't want to hurt him. "But if chemo doesn't work, if I die…" She wasn't afraid of death, but she was terrified of the hurt it would cause him.

"Then I'll have been with you through it all and

count myself lucky. Because then at least I have the memories, the imprint of you on my soul."

Her heart felt tight in her chest at those words. It seemed impossible to try to shove him away again when all she wanted was to pull him close and hug him to her.

"God put me on Mt. Rainier, Val. I truly believe that," he said, looking into her eyes.

"I believe that, too," she whispered.

At first she had thought they had found each other up there so she could help him, but perhaps she needed help, too, and just hadn't realized it. She'd been alone for so long, since her parents died, really. With Jonah, it was the first time since then that she truly felt like she was with family.

He moved a step closer and her heart thumped hard. "I'm broken—I know that—but you have helped me so much. More than I can say. And I want to be here to help you, too, if you'll let me. I have the wisdom to know that I can't change this and I can't fix it, but I can be by your side through it. That's all I want to do. I know it might sound crazy, but I love you."

Val wiped a tear from her eye. "I love you, too."

Jonah smiled. Hearing those words from Val made his heart feel lighter than he'd imagined possible only a few days before.

"Then let's go to your appointment?" he asked, offering her his hand.

She took it. The warmth of her fingers interlaced with his soothed his soul like nothing he'd ever felt. He waited for her to lead the way.

"But wait," she said, shaking her head.

He had a moment of fear. Perhaps she would still make him leave. He would if she asked him to, even though everything in him protested at the idea.

"How did you even know I was going to be here?" she asked.

He let out his breath in relief. "Clay told me."

She raised an eyebrow. "I told him not to help you contact me," she said.

She was smiling too much to be angry, but it still seemed important to clarify. "Actually, what you told him was to not give me your number or to give you messages. He didn't, but he could see how much we liked each other and thought that maybe you'd be willing to give me a chance to be here with you. He did make me promise that if you told me to go, I would go without argument. Do you want me to go?"

She seemed to consider this. "No," she said at last. "I want you to stay."

His heart jumped with happiness. Then her face got serious, though her eyes still sparkled with humor as she pointed a finger at him. "But you and Clay are both on thin ice, got it?"

He laughed. He was going to love spending his life with this feisty woman. "Got it. Won't happen again." He crossed his heart just to seal the deal.

She nodded and looked satisfied.

"So, appointment?" he prompted.

"I was going to go back to my car and grab a sweater. It's cold in here," she said.

Still holding her hand, he dug his other one into the cloth bag and pulled out a red knit sweater. "I brought this for you, just in case," he said. "It was Becca's. I think she'd like to be a part of this," he added.

The look on Val's face was all he needed to know he'd made the right choice there. He handed it to her and she draped it over her purse. "Thank you," she said, her voice soft.

"Of course," he said. They began to walk toward the elevators. After a couple of steps, Val noticed his limp. "Oh, your ankle!" she exclaimed. "You shouldn't be walking on it, Jonah."

He shrugged. "It's mostly healed. I promise I'll put it up on a chair or something. Okay?"

She thought about arguing, he could tell. "Okay," she said at last. "Coming here with an injured ankle," she mumbled, shaking her head.

"It was the only way I could be sure to find you," he protested. "Besides, we're in a hospital. This seems like the best place to be with an injured ankle."

She laughed. "Fair enough. Let's go, but carefully."

He followed her orders and slowly they made it to the elevators.

"Clay just told you where I was, huh?" she asked with a roll of her eyes.

He nodded. "Yeah, and completely unprompted, too. You should really be more careful who you tell your whereabouts to. Otherwise, near strangers could show up at any moment professing their love for you."

"Noted," she said, her lips pinching together to suppress laughter.

Without thinking, he leaned down and brushed his lips against hers. It just felt so right, and when she kissed back, everything in him melted. He looked into her eyes. "Your friends care for you, and they could see that I do, too. I can't wait to spend my life with you, if you'll let me," he told her.

"Deal," she said back.

Jonah straightened back up. "Then let's do this," he said. "You don't want to be late for your appointment."

She nodded. "I do like crosswords," she told him.

"Great," he said. "I've got enough for months. I've already discussed the situation with my work, so they know I'll be out a lot for a while."

"That's awfully flexible of them," she commented as they started toward the elevator.

"Well, when I explained that the woman I plan on marrying is starting chemotherapy, they were very understanding."

She stopped and stared at him. "Marrying?" she repeated.

He squeezed her hand. "Not right this second. But, you know, eventually. When you're ready," he said.

Val grinned at him and he grinned back. They probably looked like a couple of fools staring at each other like that, but he didn't care. He'd found the person he wanted to spend every moment with.

Thank You, God, for giving me this, he said in silent prayer.

He knew there would be difficult times ahead, but he couldn't be anything but grateful.

The elevator doors opened and they walked into it together, still smiling.

Epilogue

Jonah and Val stood close together, arms wrapped around each other, looking out at the view before them. "It's amazing, isn't it?" Jonah asked her.

Val just nodded, and he smiled. He knew by the expression on her face that she was near tears, but that they were the happy kind. The cold wind swept around them, biting at his cheeks and nose, but he felt nothing but a warm glow all the way through him as he soaked in her beauty.

"It took a few years, but I knew we'd make it up here eventually," Jonah said, giving her a little squeeze before looking again at the panorama before him. The sun was still low, the day early, and the world stretched out below where they stood on the summit of Mt. Rainier. The Cascade mountain range spread before them and off into the distance.

It was a view worth every step it had taken to get there.

Jonah reached into the small container at their feet and pulled out a tattered book, and they signed their names side by side on one line. Val added a little heart to it, which made Jonah smile. Then they put it away and continued to look at the gorgeous view.

"I thought you said it was going to be foggy today and the view probably wouldn't be great up here," Val said, raising an eyebrow at Jonah.

"I was definitely wrong. This is one of the most beautiful summit views I've ever seen," he conceded, squeezing her close.

"And there were zero whiteouts or mountain lions this time," she added. "So that's nice."

He grinned. "We have the hike down, so there's still another chance for peril."

Val shrugged her shoulders. "At least those things we know we can handle no problem. Mountain lions and a bit of snow? No big deal. So long as we avoid the hordes of marmots plotting our demise."

Jonah laughed. "Wouldn't want to run into those," he agreed.

He watched Val smile up at him and thanked God for every moment he had had with her over the past six years. He leaned down and kissed her. She smiled at him, that same sweet smile he'd seen a million times. It struck him to his heart, just like it had the first time, sitting on top of the haystack at Mt. Si.

"I love you," he said for probably the millionth time.

"I love you, too," she replied, her jade eyes sparkling up at him.

They embraced for a long moment, each of them sending a prayer of thanks up to the heavens that felt so near to the mountaintop.

"We need to get a picture of us at the summit. For Becca," Val said, her voice muffled against his jacket.

Jonah shifted away a little, just enough to pull out his phone and snap a few pictures of them. "There," he said, showing her the results. "Now she'll know we actually made it. We have proof and everything."

"So when we get home and she demands to know whether or not we managed to summit Mt. Rainier, we have evidence for her."

"I'm sure that's the first thing she'll expect when we get home. Evidence that we actually did what we've been talking about doing all this time," Jonah said. He thought of his little daughter and ached to get home to her.

"I hope she's having fun with your parents. We've never been gone so long before," Val said, looking a little anxious.

"I imagine she's standing by the door, looking at her watch and tapping her foot, waiting for us to get back," he said with a chuckle.

"That would take a lot of coordination for an eighteen-month-old," she told him.

"Her grandmother will probably have spent the whole time we've been gone teaching it to her. The women in my family have that down to an art form. It was one of my sister's specialties by the time we were in kindergarten, even though she didn't own a watch."

Val laughed. "Well then, it seems inevitable that Baby Becca will do that, too. I think she's going to be so much like your sister when she gets older."

Jonah smiled at the thought of his twin sister. There was pain there, too, and that would never go away, but he'd learned to accept it. And his daughter would grow up hearing about her namesake and the memories would stay alive in all of them, and that warmed his heart.

"I'm sure she will," Jonah agreed. "Except I think Baby Becca will probably like mountains quite a bit more than my sister did."

"Of course," Val said with a smile. "She'll be out here with us before we know it. Keeping an eye out for mountain lions and marmots."

"I can't wait to get home and tell her all about this," Jonah said.

Val nodded. "Me neither. Let's go home to our baby girl," she said as she hefted her pack onto her shoulders.

When she was ready, she held out her hand to him. He made sure his gear was settled and reached out, taking her gloved hand in his and clasping it tight.

With one last look around, they started back down, both ready to be home.

* * * * *

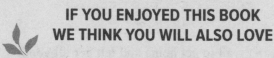

SPECIAL EXCERPT FROM

LOVE INSPIRED SUSPENSE
INSPIRATIONAL ROMANCE

*When a killer sends her taunting letters, FBI behavioral
analyst Chelsey Banks retreats to a friend's ranch—and
interrupts the housekeeper being attacked. Learning it
matches the MO of a cold-case serial killer, she'll need
to work with her best friend, Texas Ranger
Tack Holliday—unless one of the killers gets her first.*

Read on for a sneak peek of
Texas Cold Case Threat,
a new Love Inspired Suspense story by Jessica R. Patch!

"He's brazen. He parked right behind Izzy's old van
knowing there was a possibility of someone—maybe even
me—seeing it." Which she had. She could kick herself for
not getting the tag number.

"Are you saying I'm looking for an arrogant killer who
loves the thrill of almost getting caught but believes he
won't because he's uncatchable?"

Her past mistakes told her not to make a solid conclusion
so soon, but this guy had proven more than once what kind
of man he was, what kind of killer. Still, she hesitated to
give Tack a profile that would aid in his search. "Perhaps,"
she said as a knot pinched in her gut.

"Perhaps? Chelsey, give me something I can work with."

Chelsey drank the ice water, letting it cool her burning
throat. What if she was wrong? "I'm not ready to spin
what little thread we have into a tapestry yet." She could
not have another profile backfiring. Another stain on her

previously impeccable record. Lives depended on it. Tack's career depended on it. The last thing Chelsey wanted was Tack's name being smeared because of his connection with Chelsey and her profession.

Or her personal stains that could smear him.

"Agents—" a hospital security officer stepped inside "—we have a media frenzy outside. They want more information on this Outlaw. They know a woman died at his hands. In our care."

The Outlaw. Chelsey's name for him.

The only other person besides Tack who knew she'd called him that was Juan. He must have talked to the press after he left the hospital. So much for not letting their personal nickname for him get out. Now they were here wanting answers. She didn't have a single one.

"We're going to have to go out there, Chels," Tack said. "Me and you. Working a case together. Who would have thought?"

And now if anything at all were amiss, Tack would go down with an already sinking ship, in the form of his oldest and dearest friend.

What had she gotten him into? And could she get him out?

Don't miss
Texas Cold Case Threat by Jessica R. Patch,
available March 2022 wherever
Love Inspired Suspense books and ebooks are sold.

And look for a new extended-length novel from
Jessica R. Patch, Her Darkest Secret,
coming soon from Love Inspired!

LoveInspired.com

LISEXP0122B

IF YOU ENJOYED THIS BOOK, DON'T MISS NEW EXTENDED-LENGTH NOVELS FROM LOVE INSPIRED!

In addition to the Love Inspired books you know and love, we're excited to introduce even more uplifting stories in a longer format, with more inspiring fresh starts and page-turning thrills!

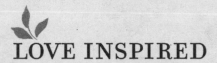

LOVE INSPIRED

Stories to uplift and inspire.

Fall in love with Love Inspired—inspirational and uplifting stories of faith and hope. Find strength and comfort in the bonds of friendship and community. Revel in the warmth of possibility, and the promise of new beginnings.

LOOK FOR THESE LOVE INSPIRED TITLES ONLINE AND IN THE BOOK DEPARTMENT OF YOUR FAVORITE RETAILER!